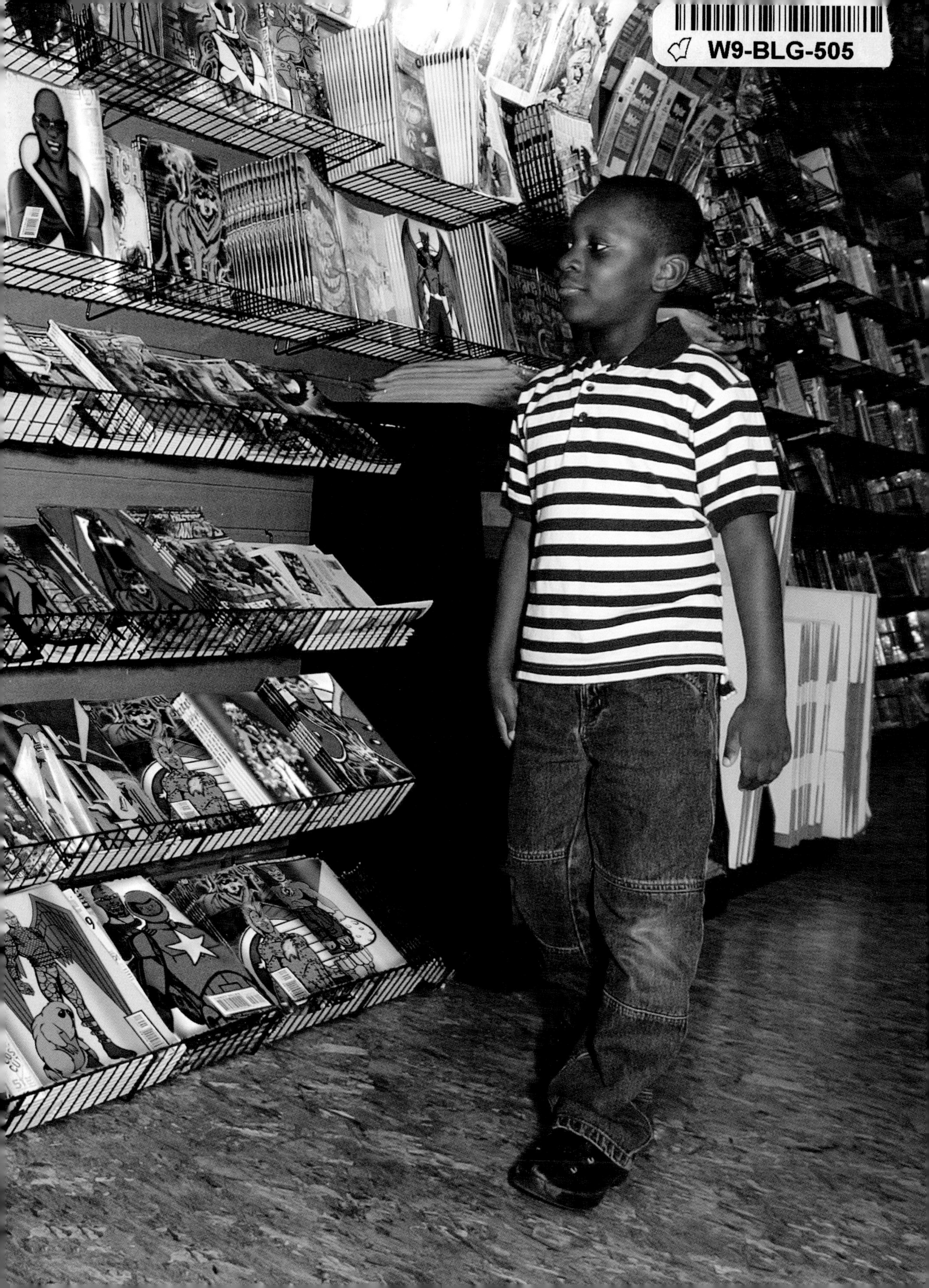

To Malik

A special thanks to Paul Colin and Jeff Amato, and also to Midtown Comics NYC for the use of their location. Bandai's Tetsujin 28go and Gundam toys on pages 8, 36, and 37 are used with permission from Bandai America Incorporated.

LIBRARY OF CONGRESS CATALOGING-IN-PUBLICATION DATA

Tauss, Marc. ▪ Superhero / by Marc Tauss.— 1st ed. ▪ p.   cm. ▪ Summary: Maleek and his robot Marvyn travel to the past to find trees and plants to restore the city that tall buildings have taken over. ▪ ISBN 0-439-62734-6 (hardcover) [1. Heroes—Fiction. 2. Time travel—Fiction. 3. Robots—Fiction.] I. Title. ▪ PZ7.T211426Su 2005   [E]—dc22   2004025034

12 11 10 9 8 7 6 5 4 3 2 1   05 06 07 08 09

Printed in Singapore   46 ▪ First edition, September 2005

The text type was set in DINEngschrift ▪ Book design by Marijka Kostiw

MARC TAUSS

SUPER HERO

SCHOLASTIC PRESS ▪ NEW YORK

Maleek loved comic books.

It was fun to catch up on his fellow superheroes' adventures.

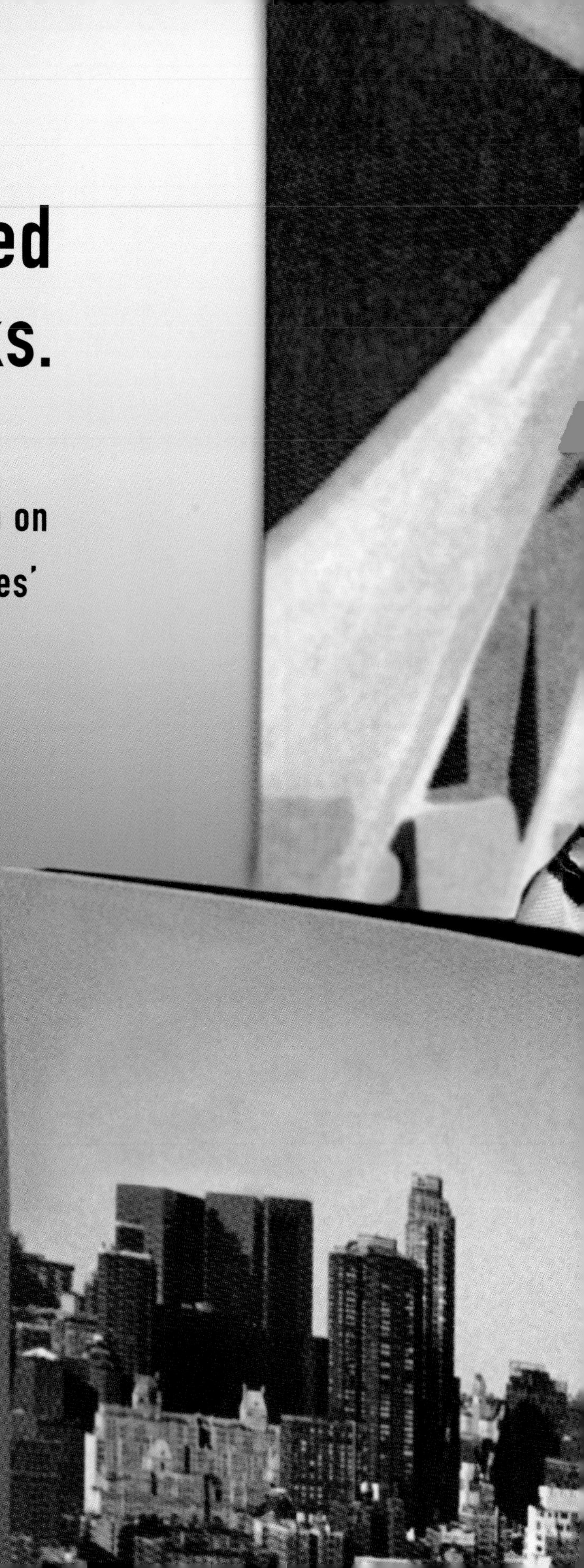

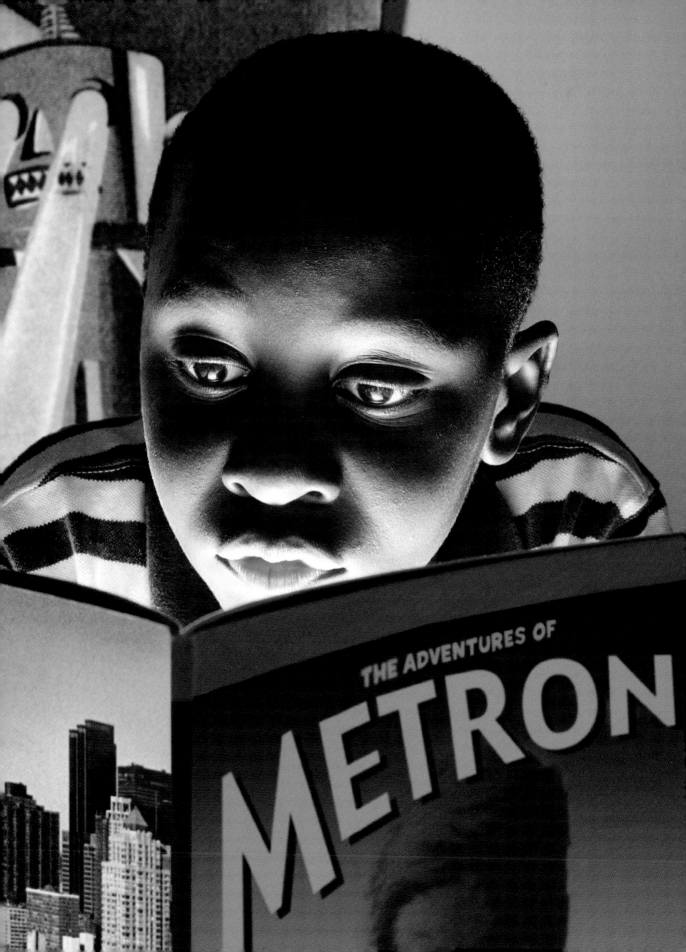

THE ADVENTURES OF
METRON

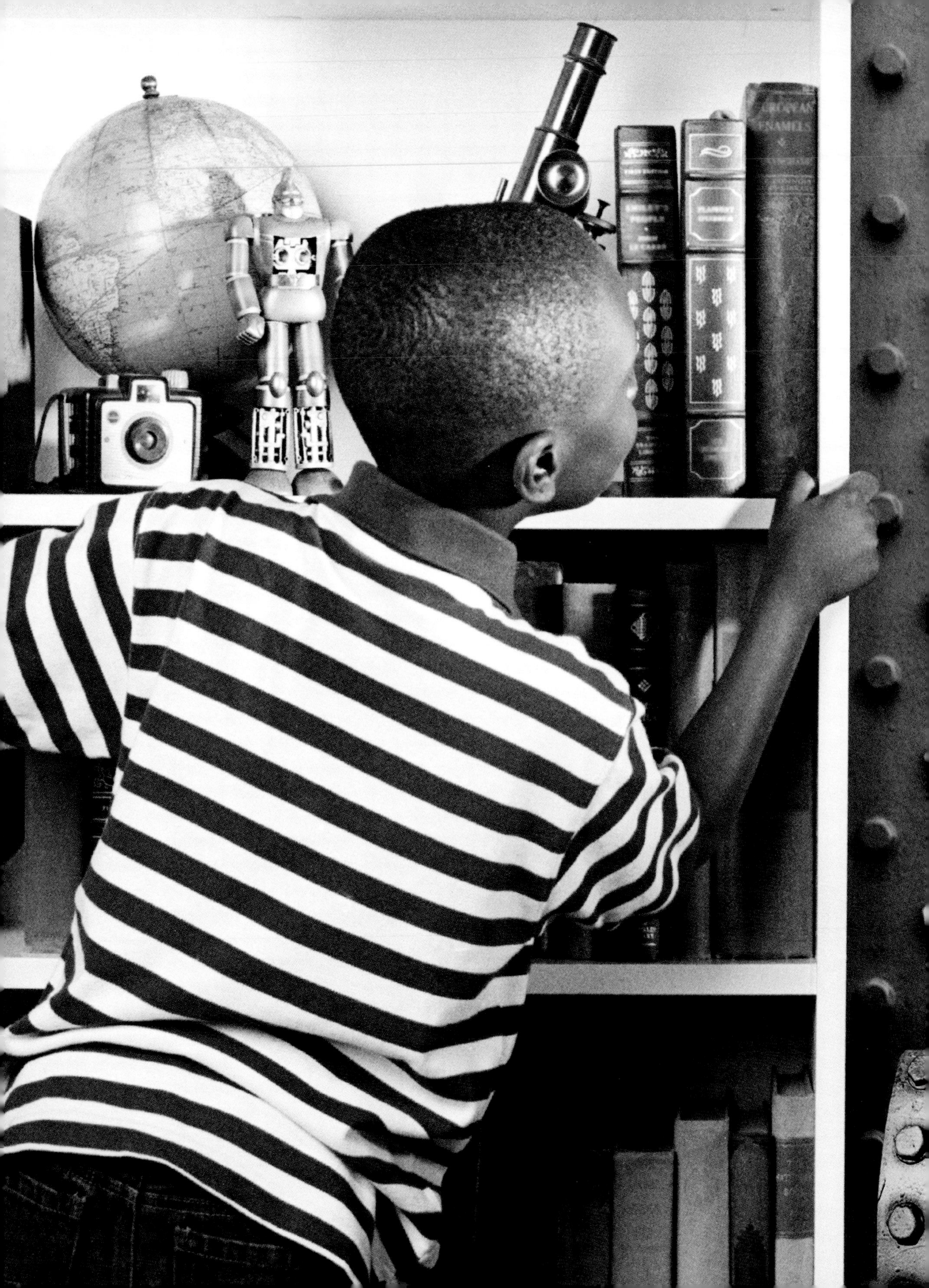

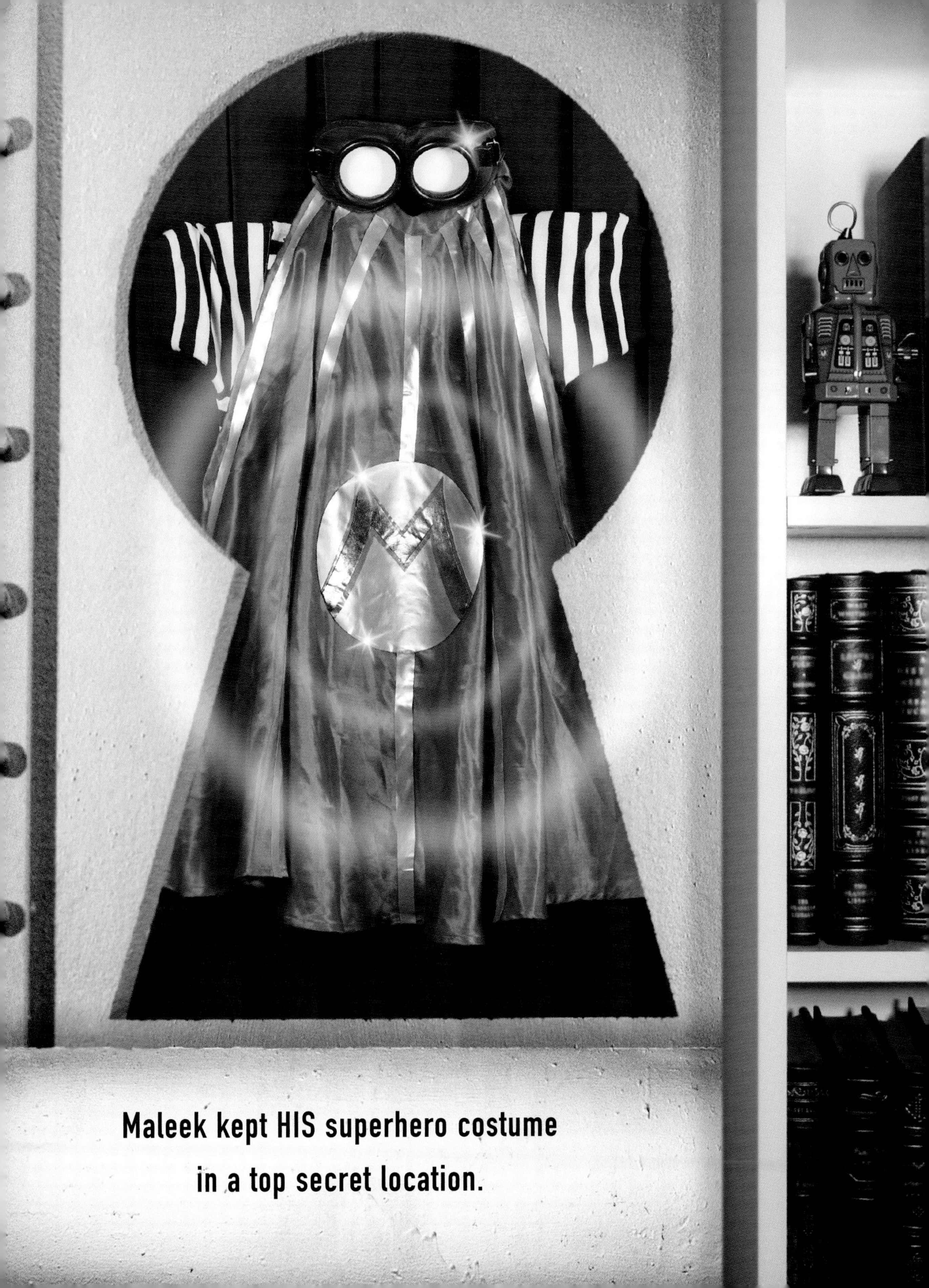

Maleek kept HIS superhero costume
in a top secret location.

It concealed his identity when
he went out to do his
top secret work.

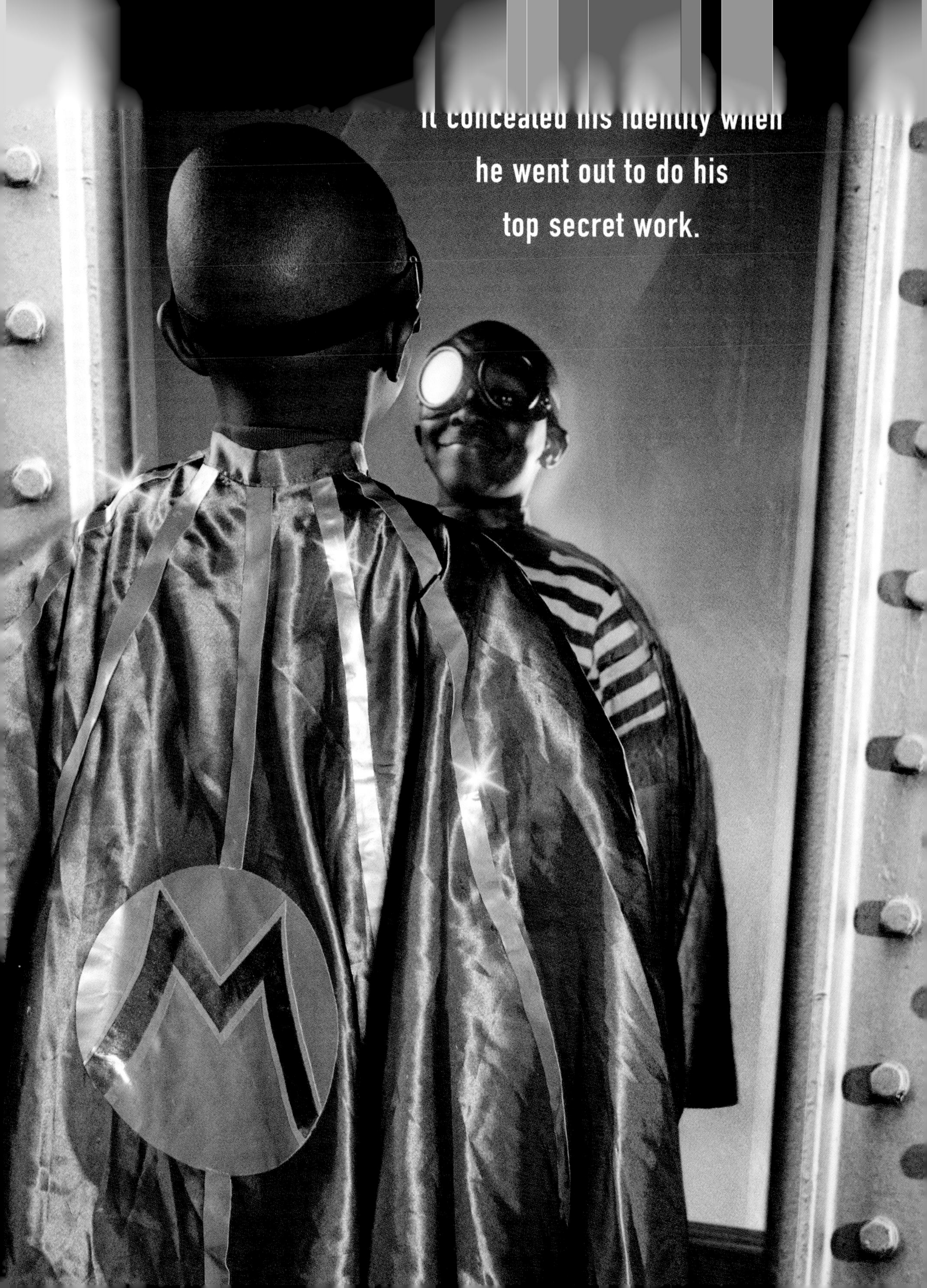

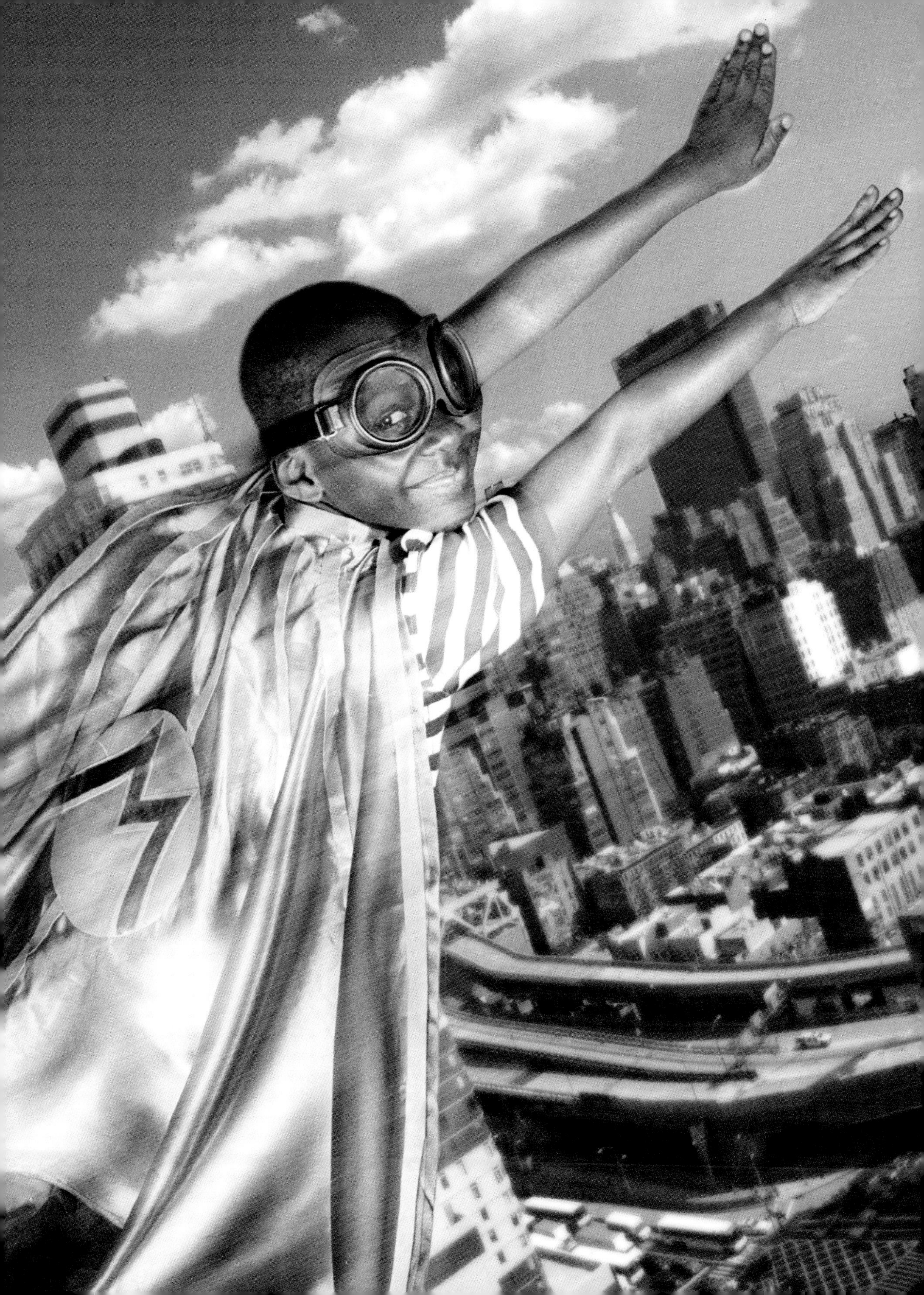

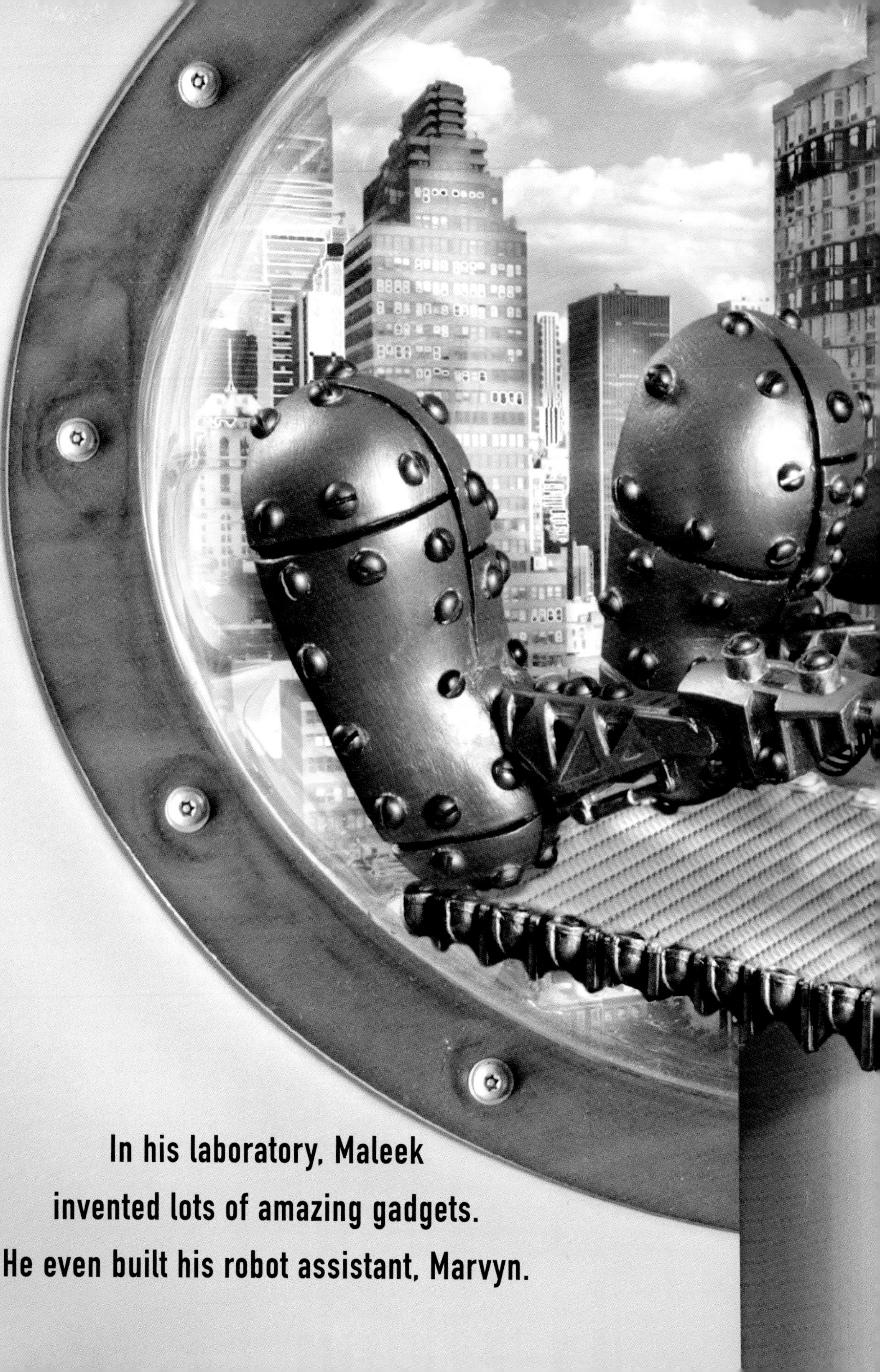

In his laboratory, Maleek
invented lots of amazing gadgets.
He even built his robot assistant, Marvyn.

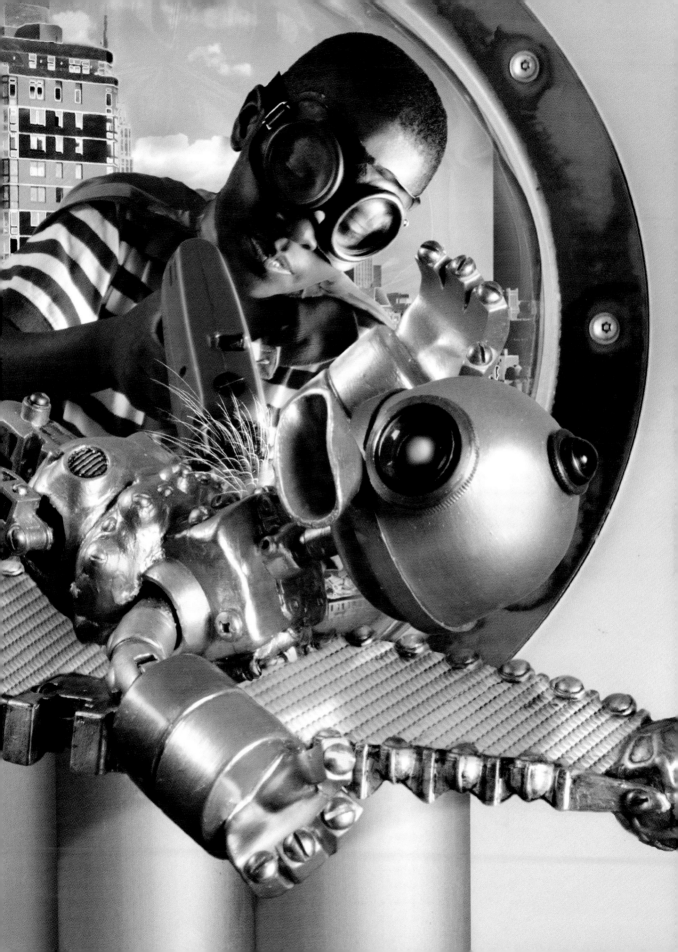

One morning, Maleek
awoke to urgent news.

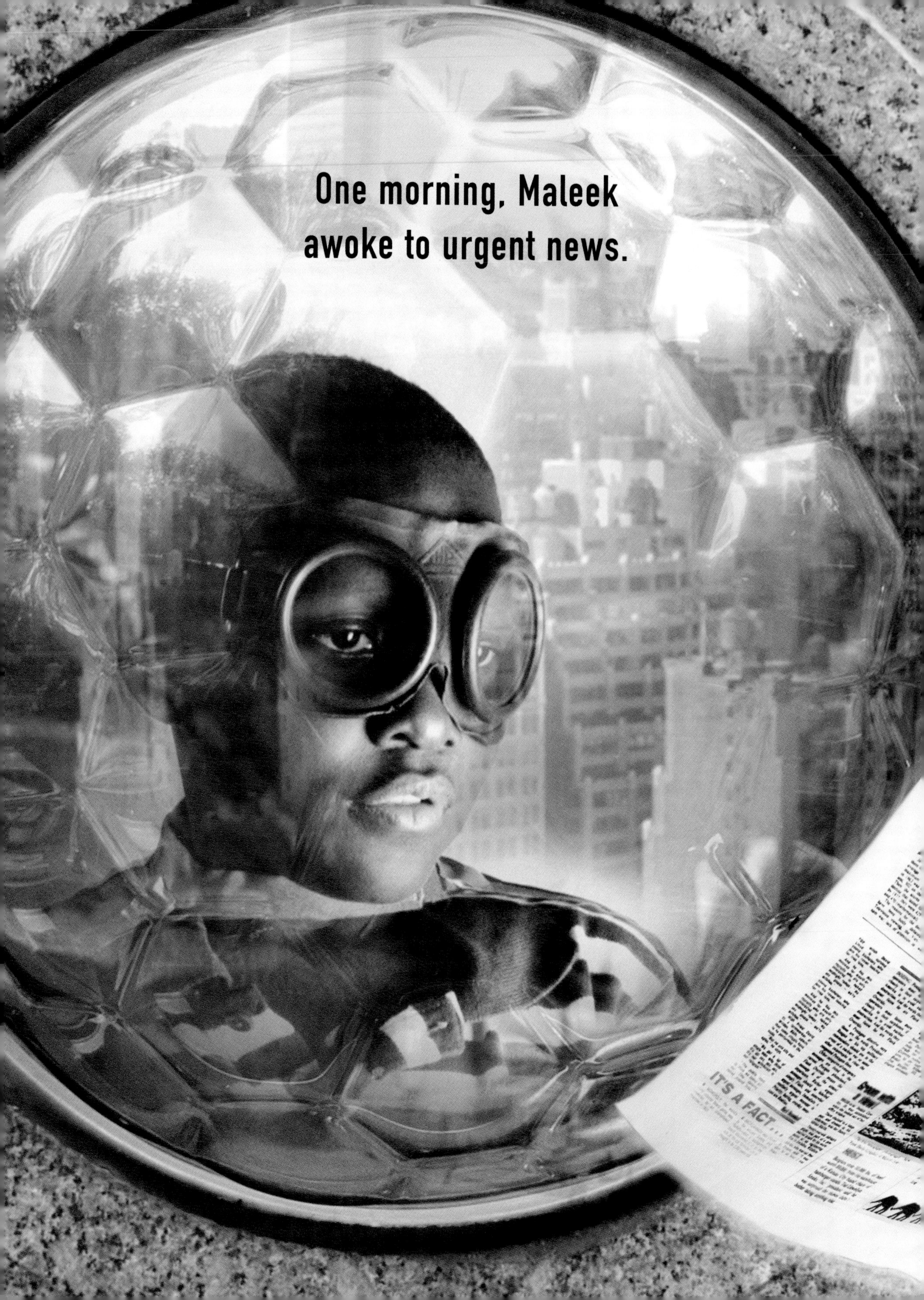
IT'S A FACT...

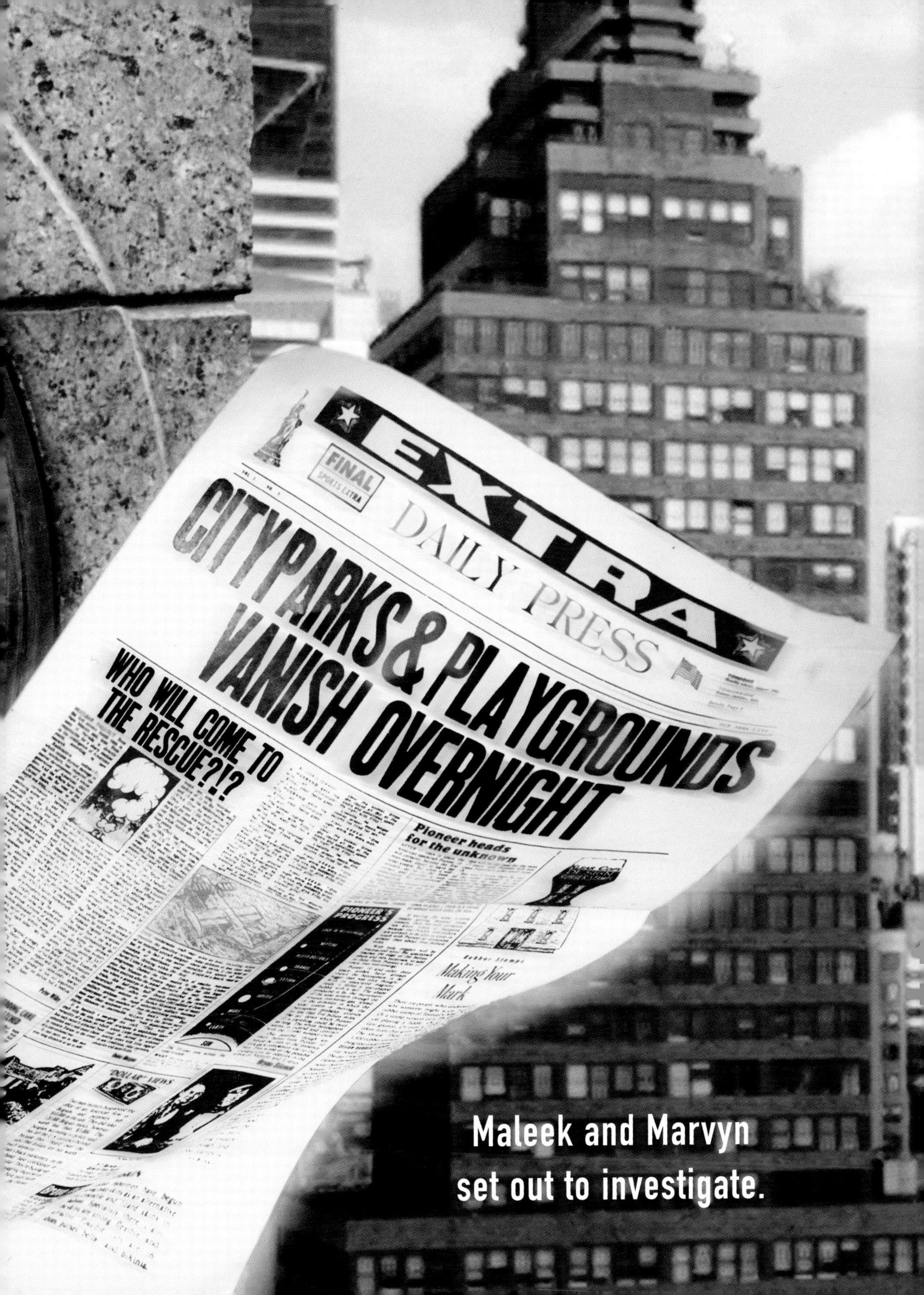
EXTRA
DAILY PRESS
FINAL
SPORTS EXTRA
CITY PARKS & PLAYGROUNDS VANISH OVERNIGHT
WHO WILL COME TO THE RESCUE?!?
Pioneer heads for the unknown
PIONEER'S PROGRESS
Making Your Mark

Maleek and Marvyn
set out to investigate.

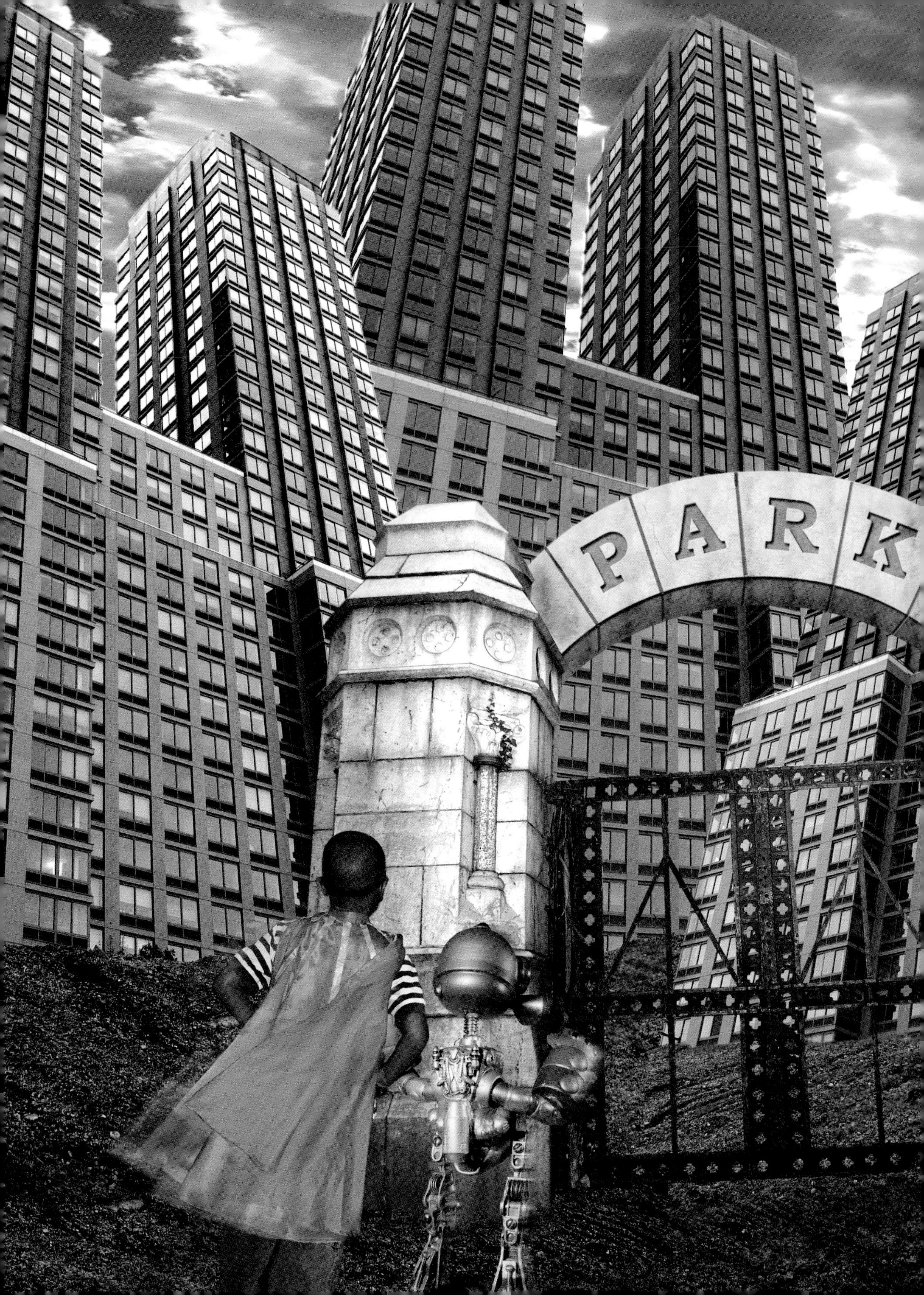
PARK

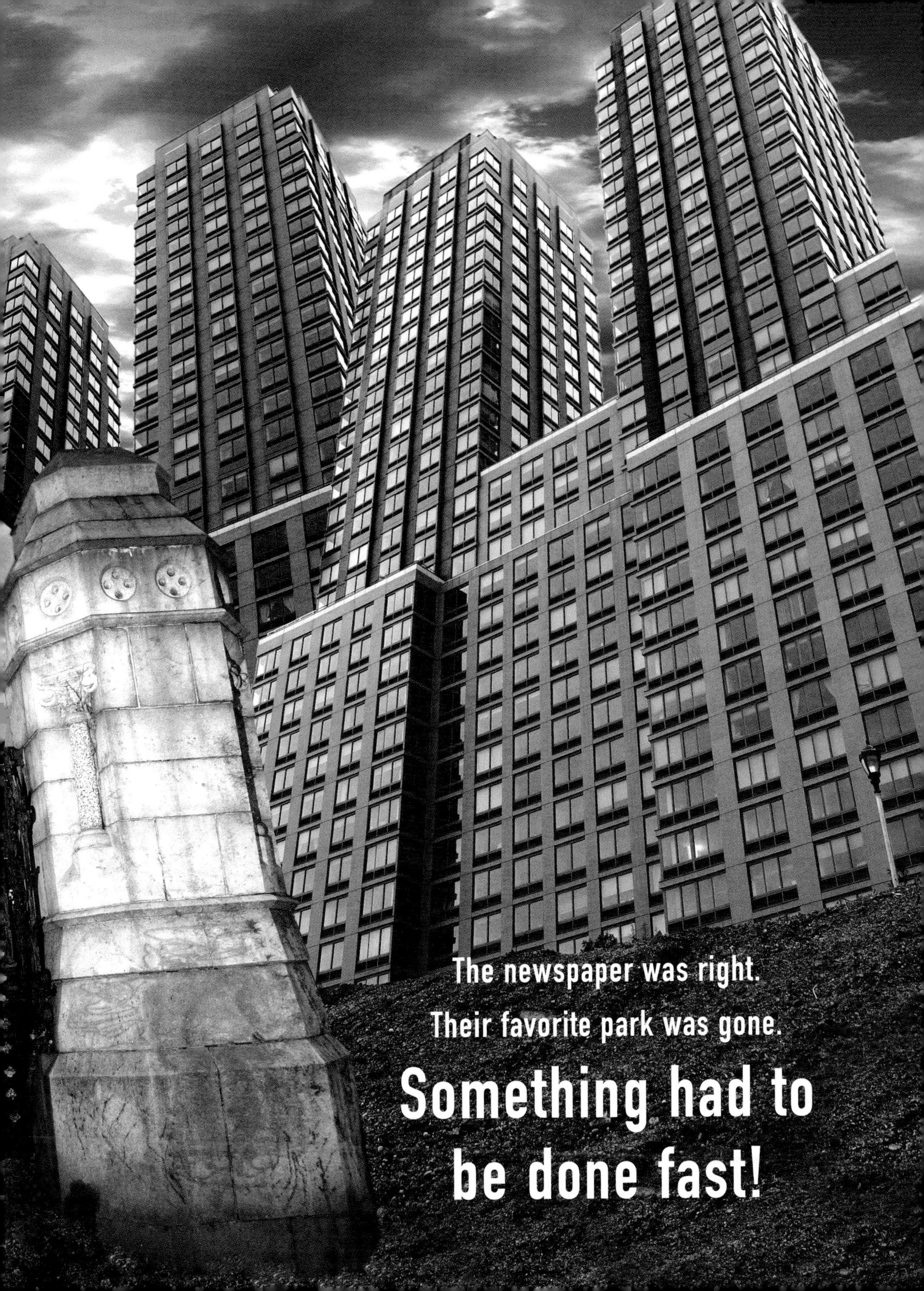

The newspaper was right.
Their favorite park was gone.

Something had to be done fast!

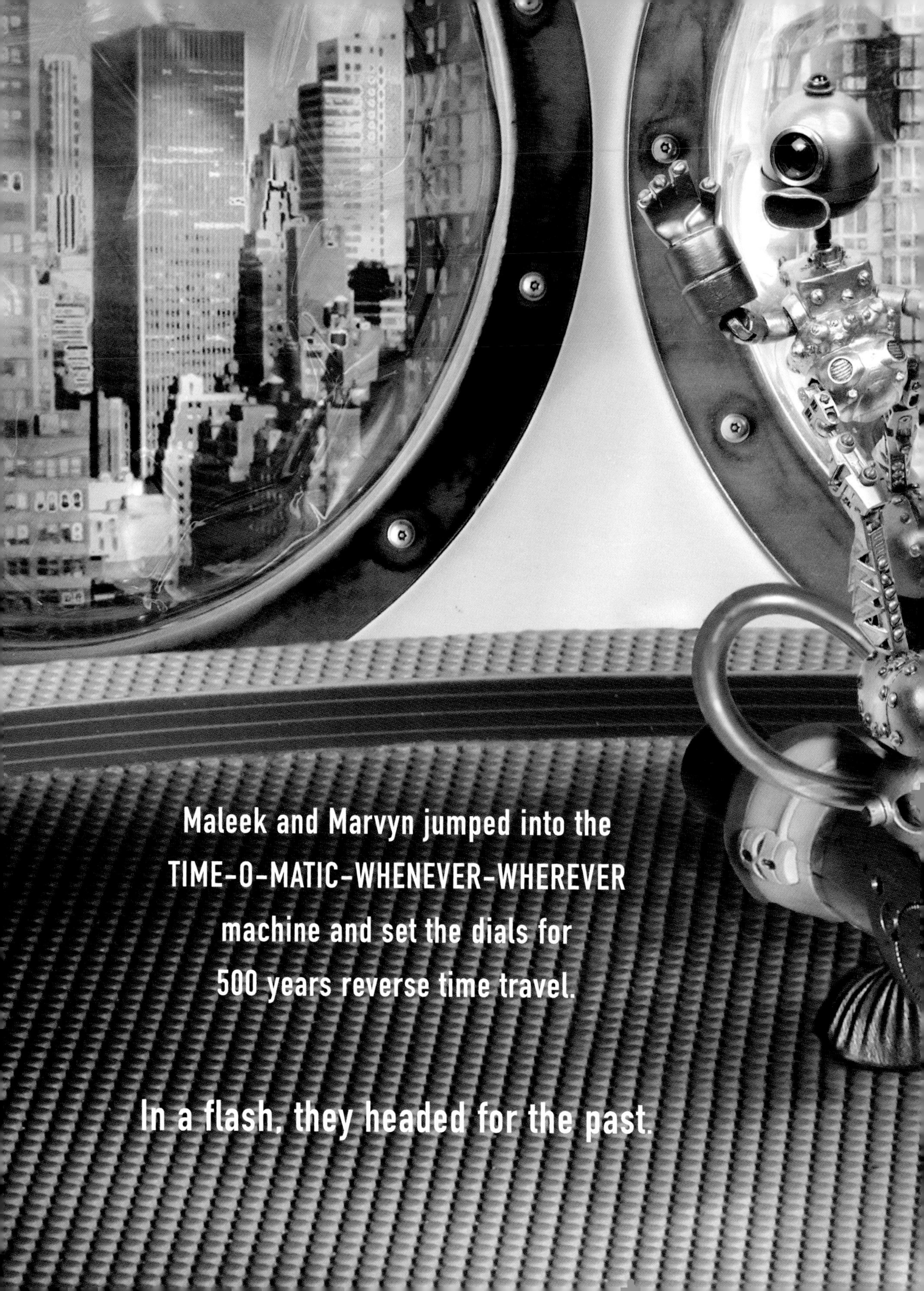

Maleek and Marvyn jumped into the TIME-O-MATIC-WHENEVER-WHEREVER machine and set the dials for 500 years reverse time travel.

In a flash, they headed for the past.

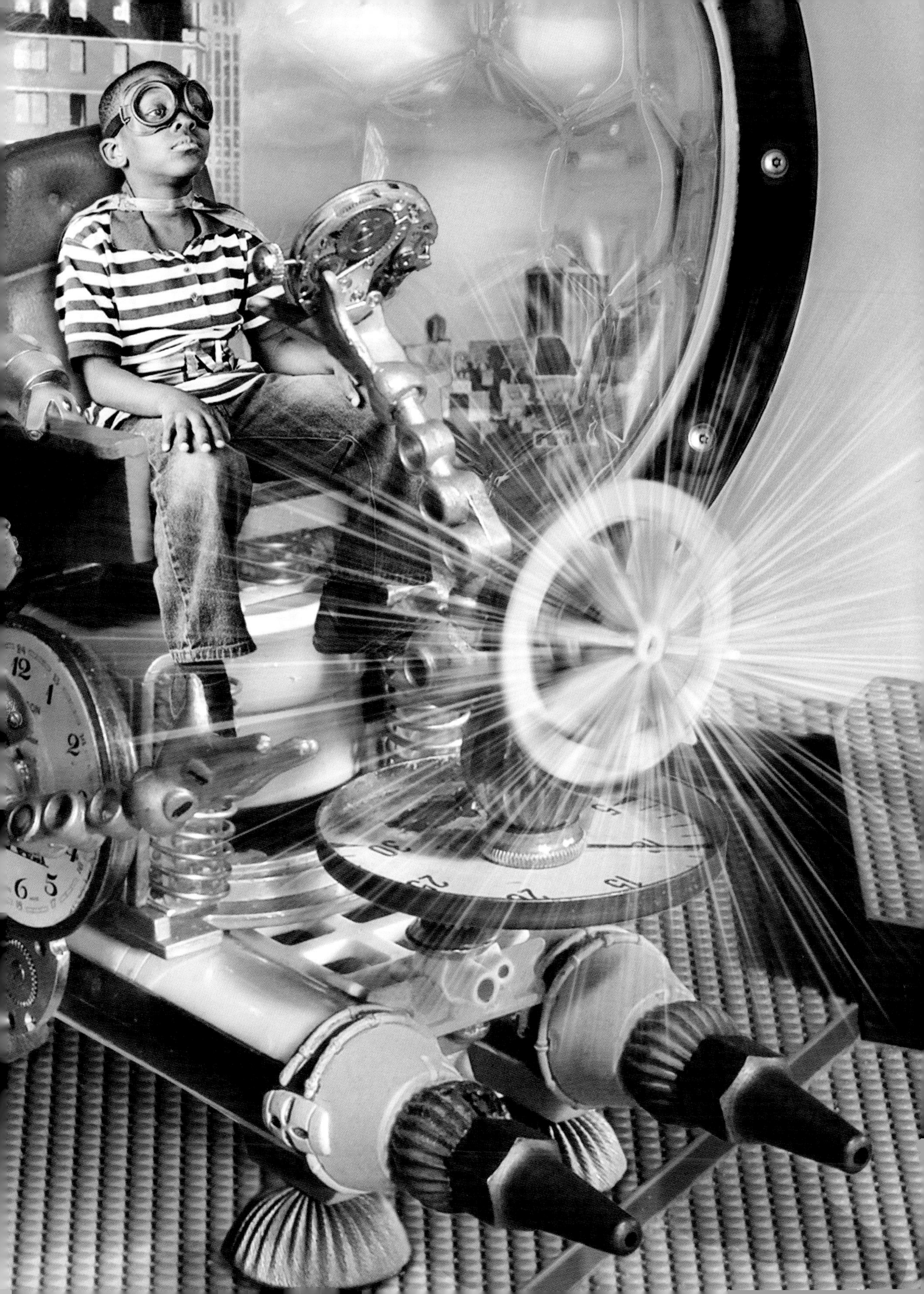

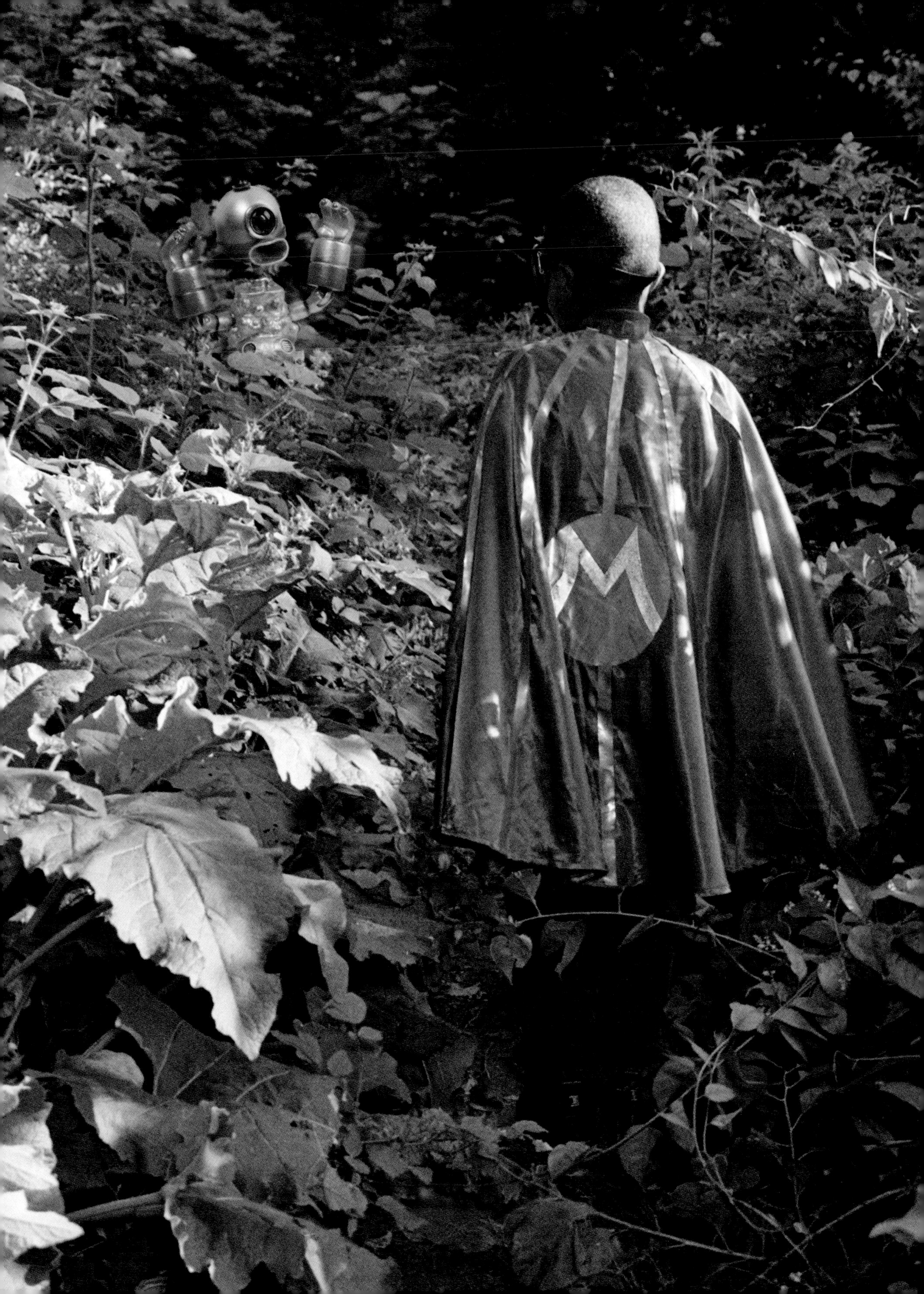

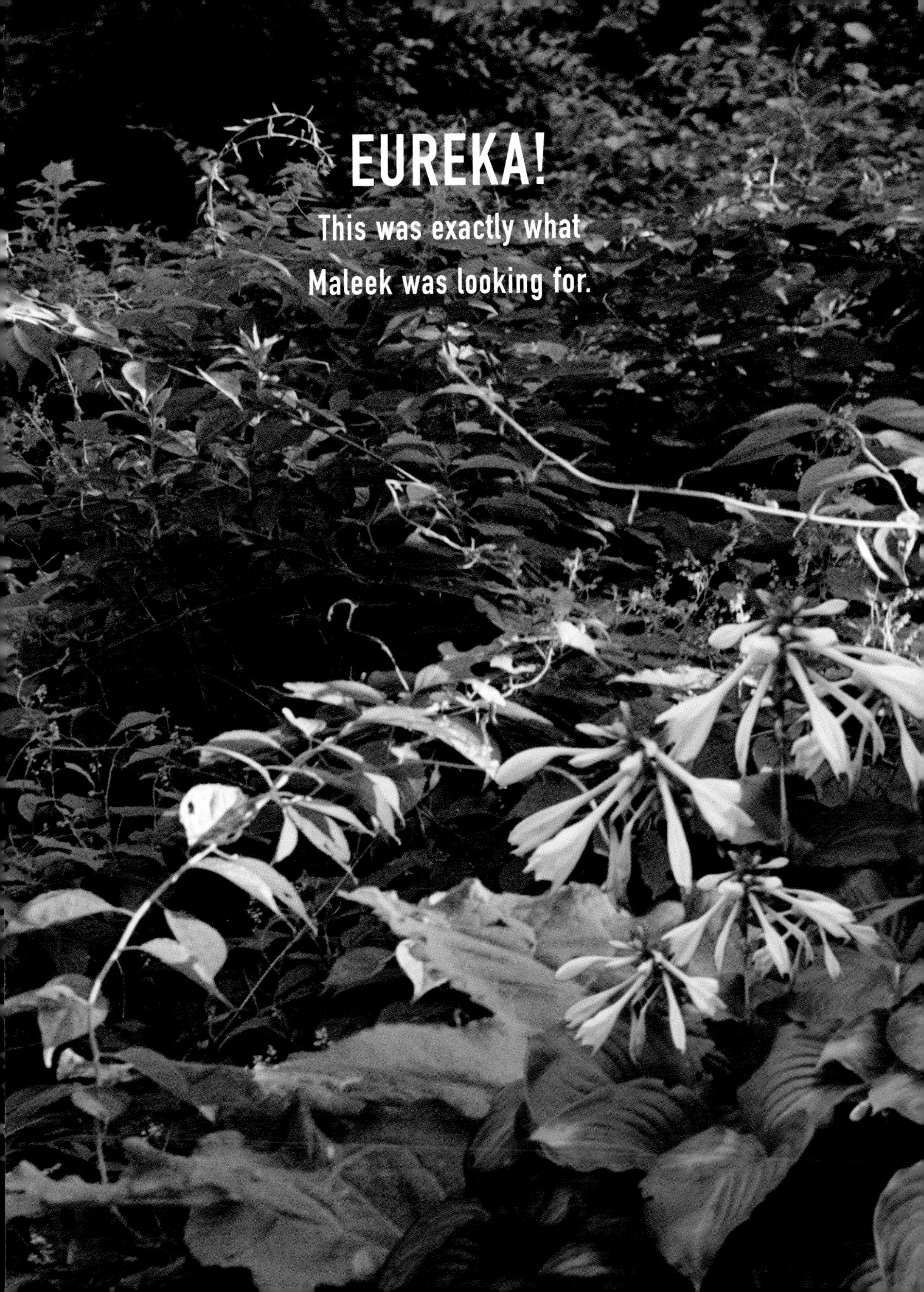

EUREKA!

This was exactly what Maleek was looking for.

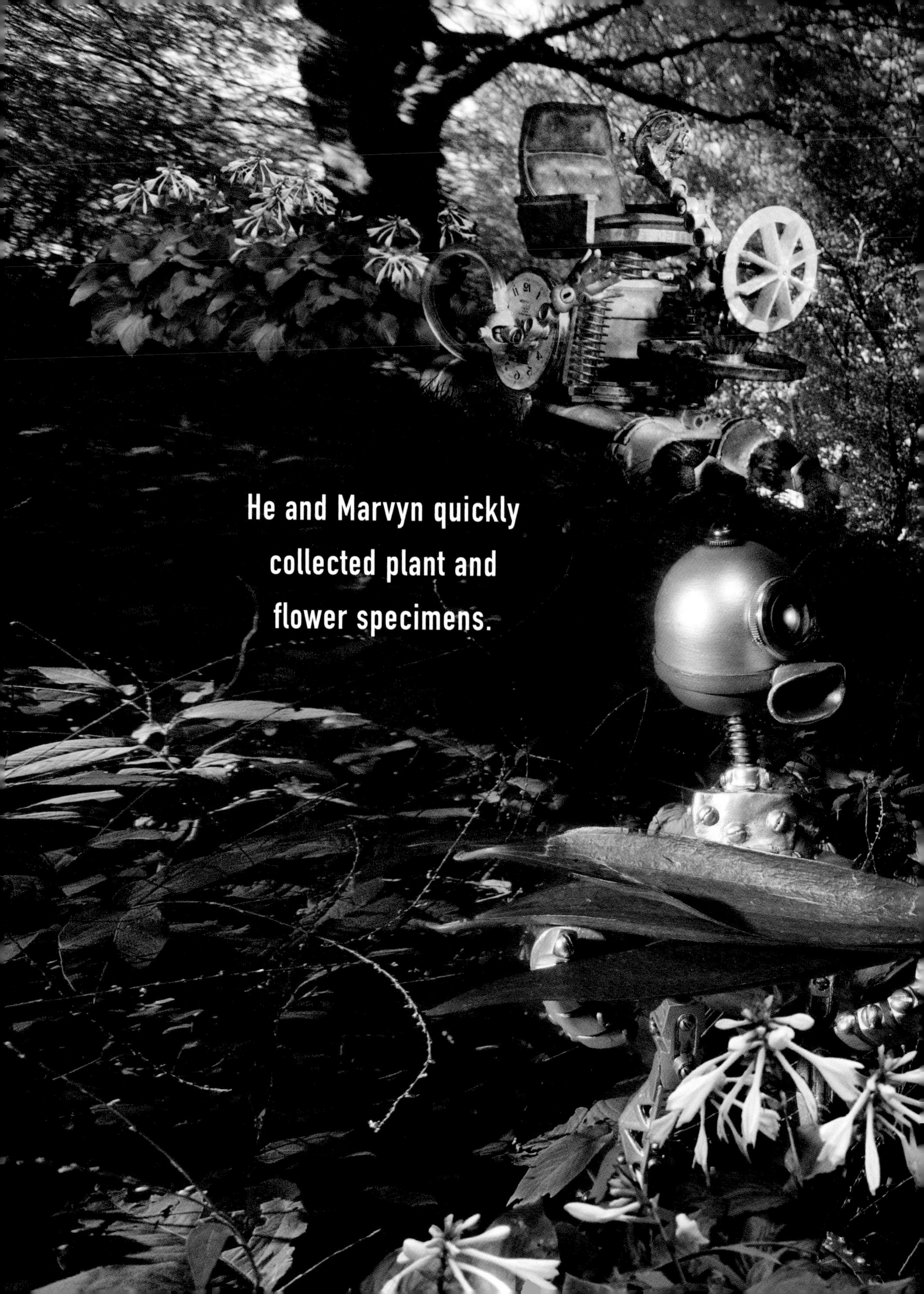

He and Marvyn quickly
collected plant and
flower specimens.

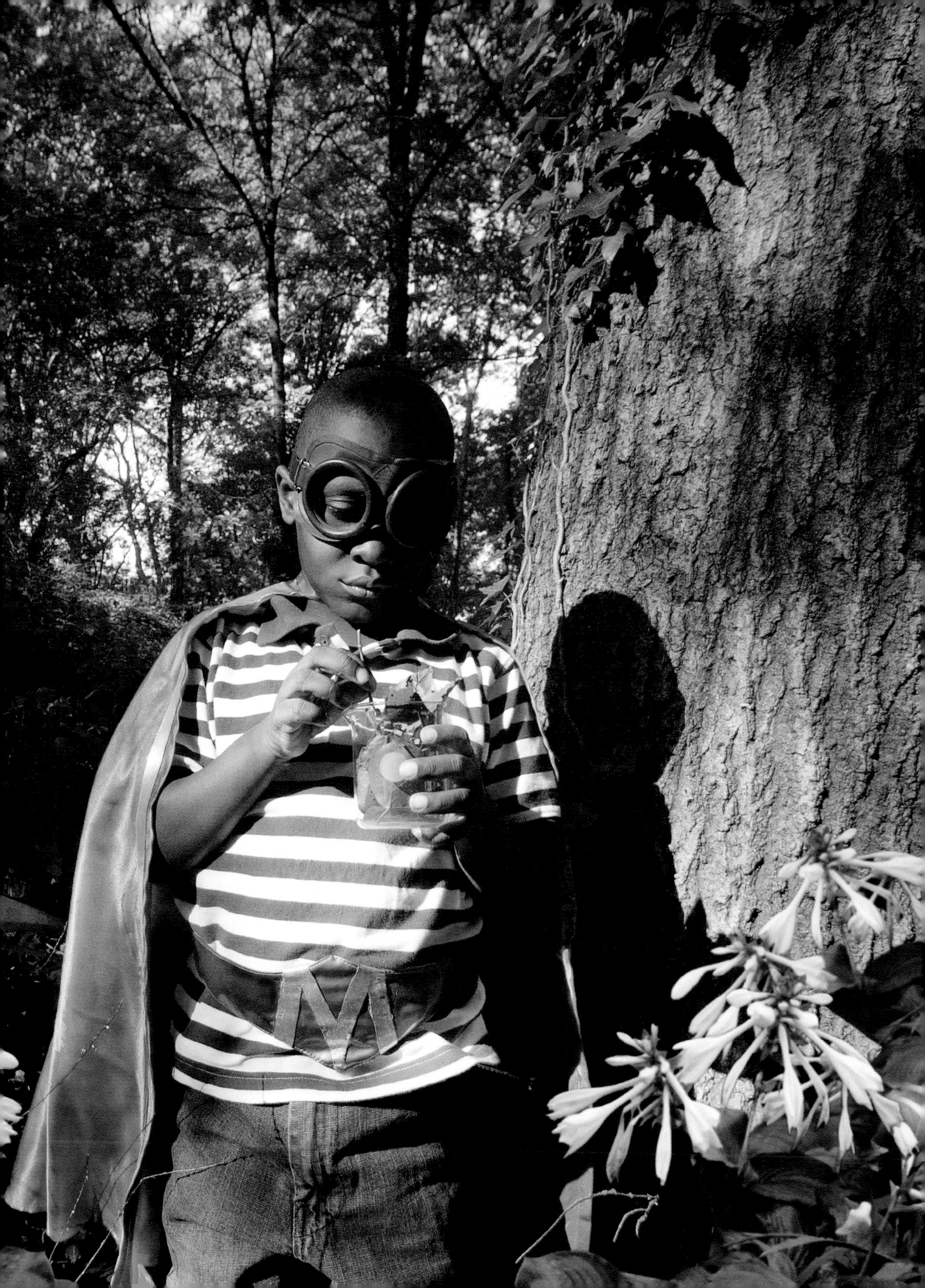

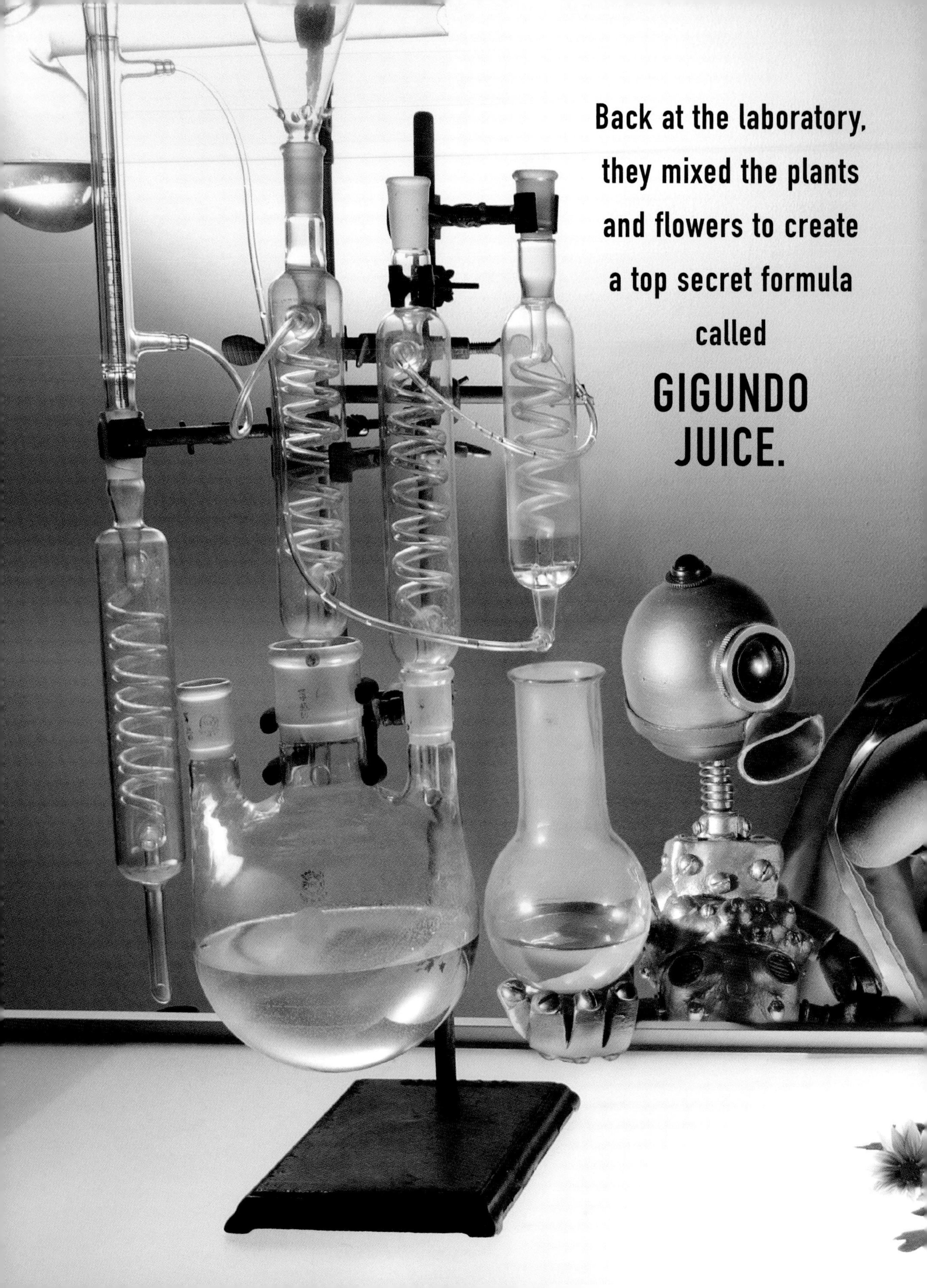

Back at the laboratory, they mixed the plants and flowers to create a top secret formula called

GIGUNDO JUICE.

Could this be the answer?

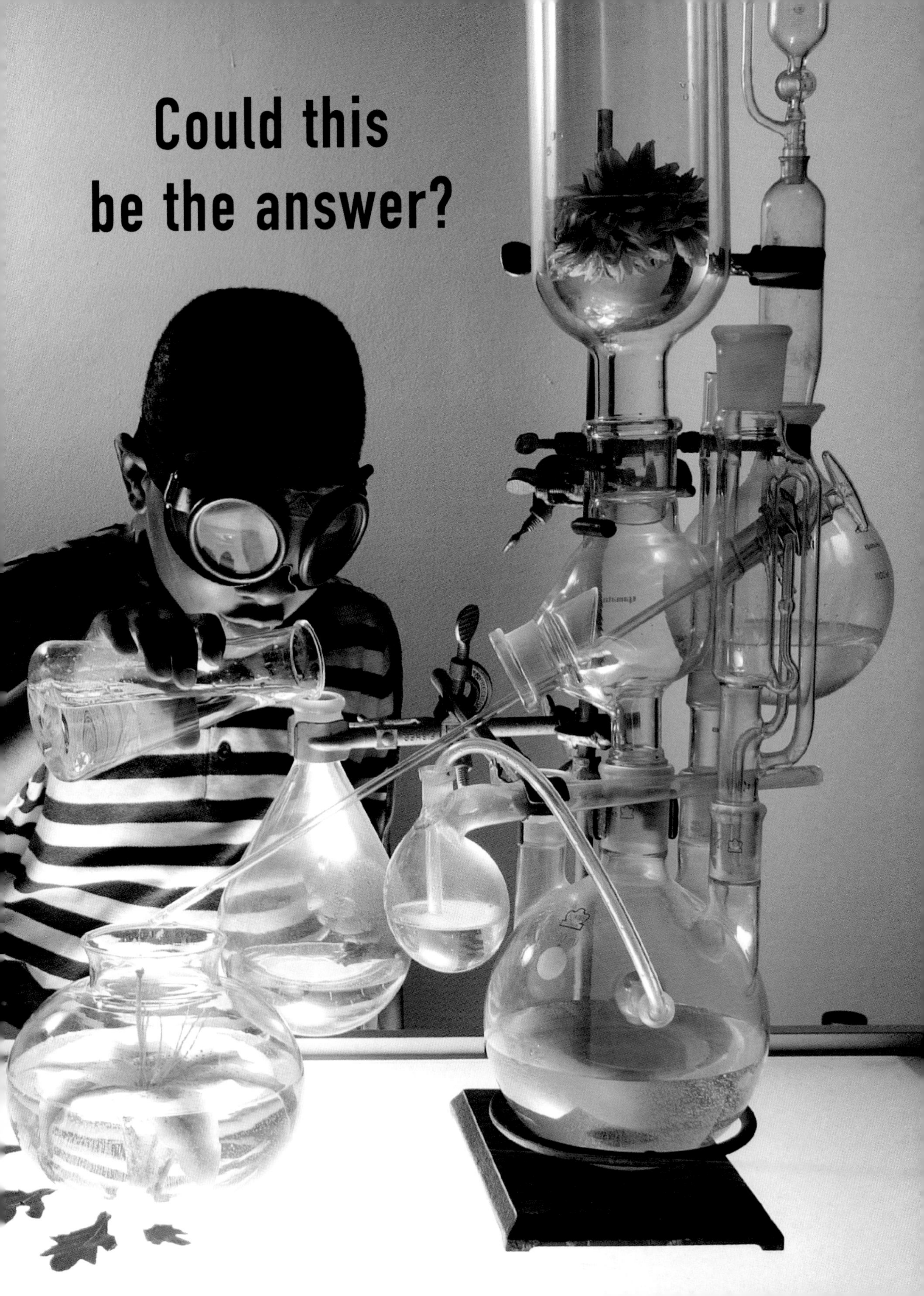

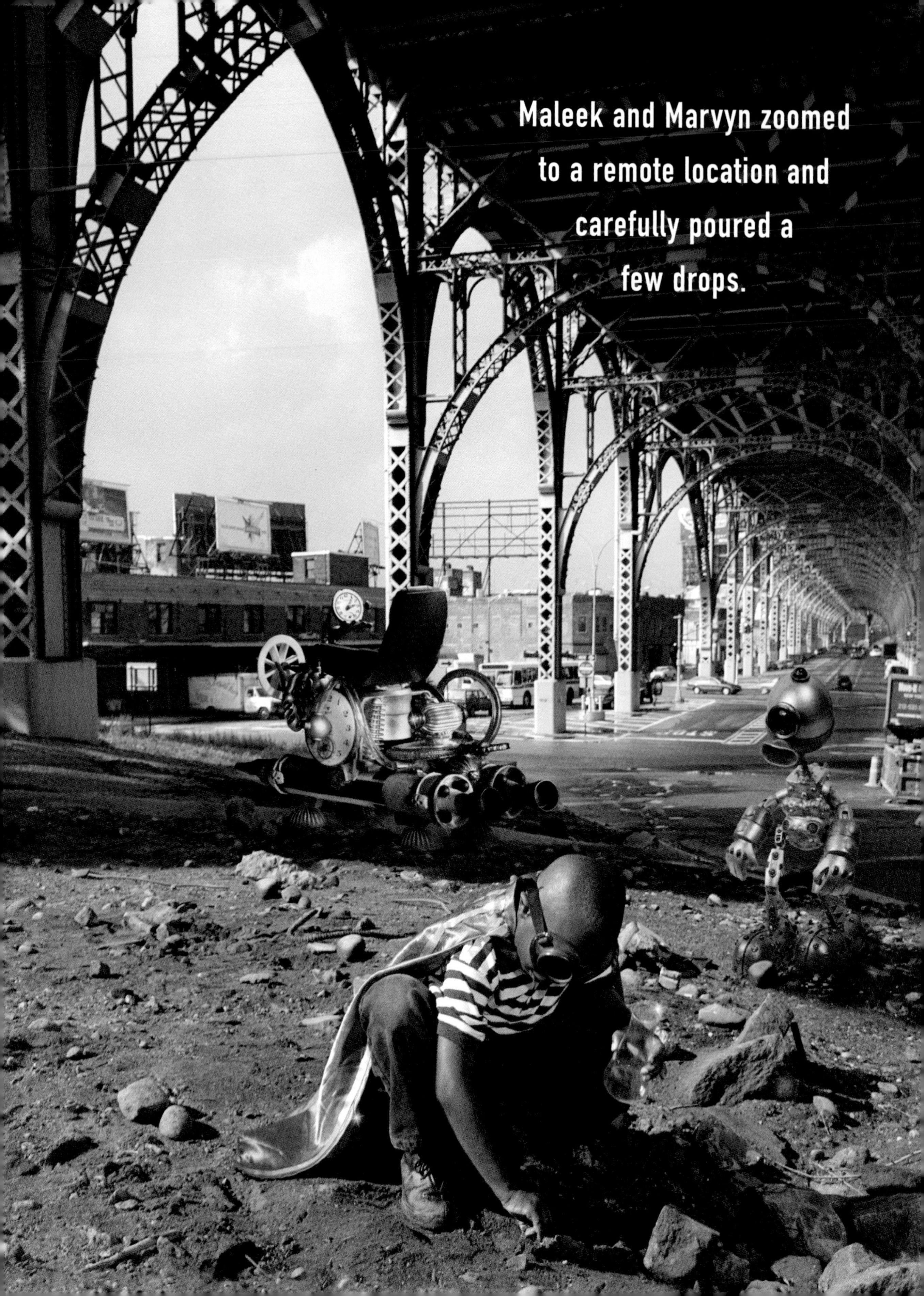

Maleek and Marvyn zoomed to a remote location and carefully poured a few drops.

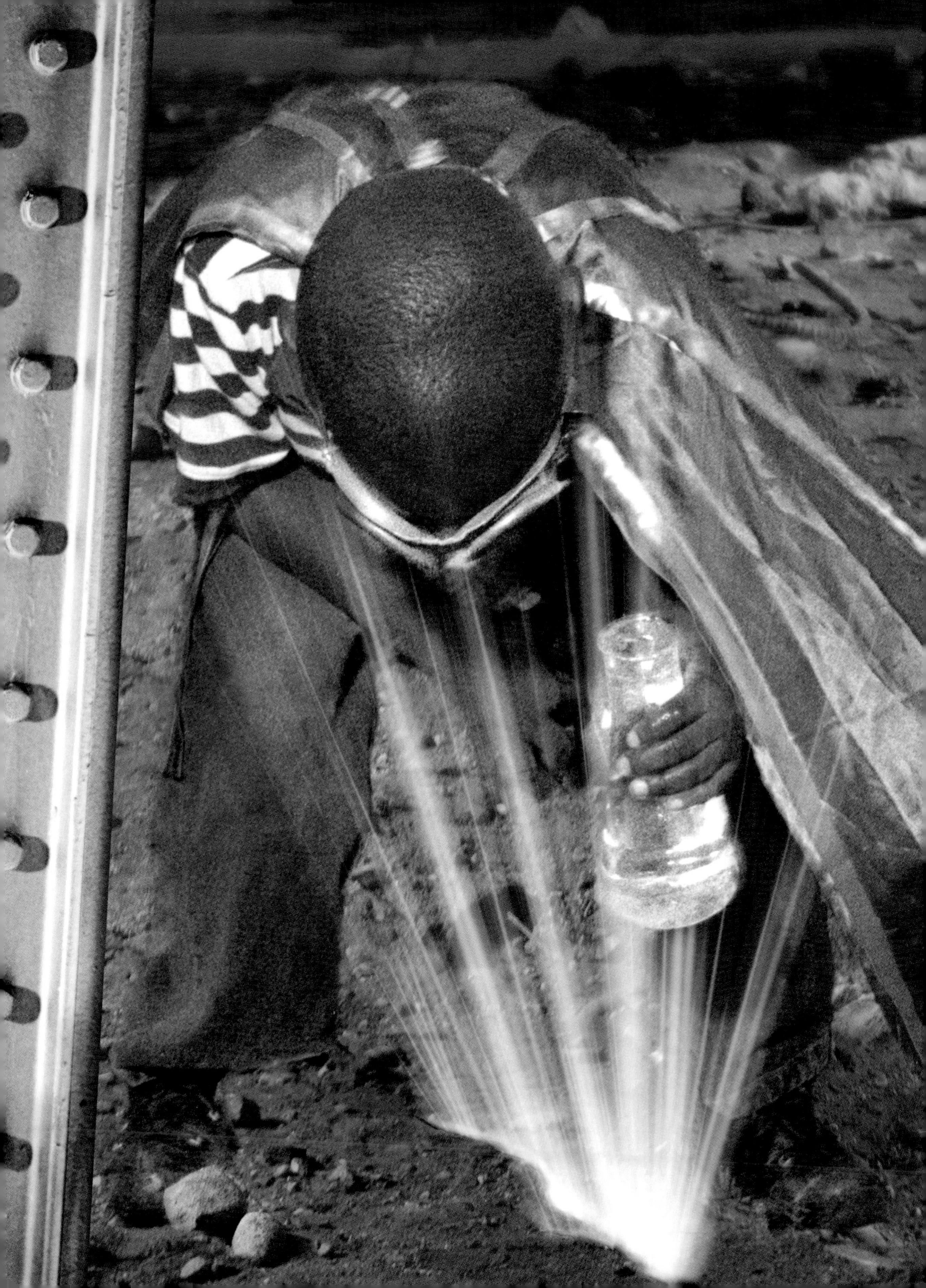

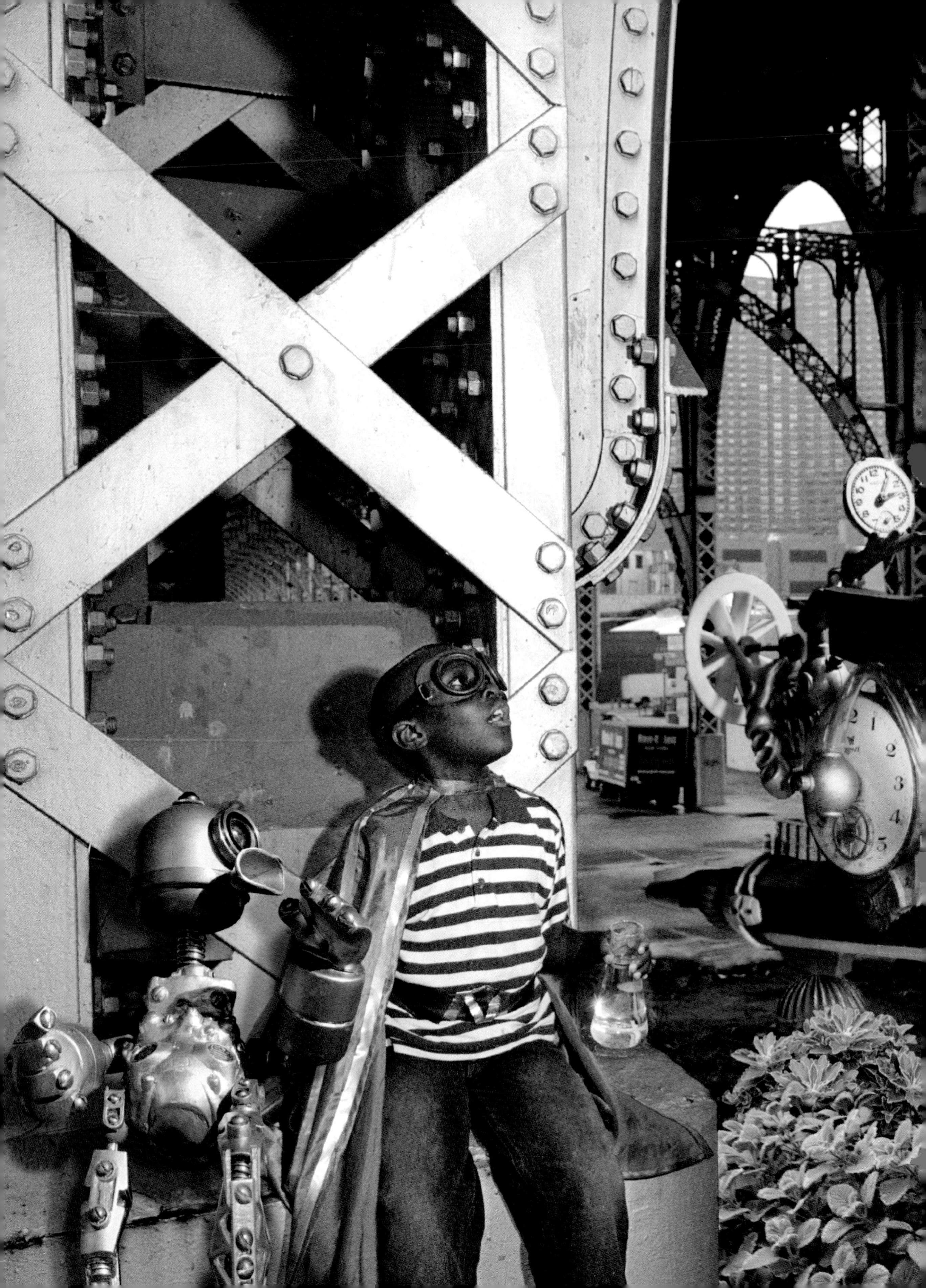

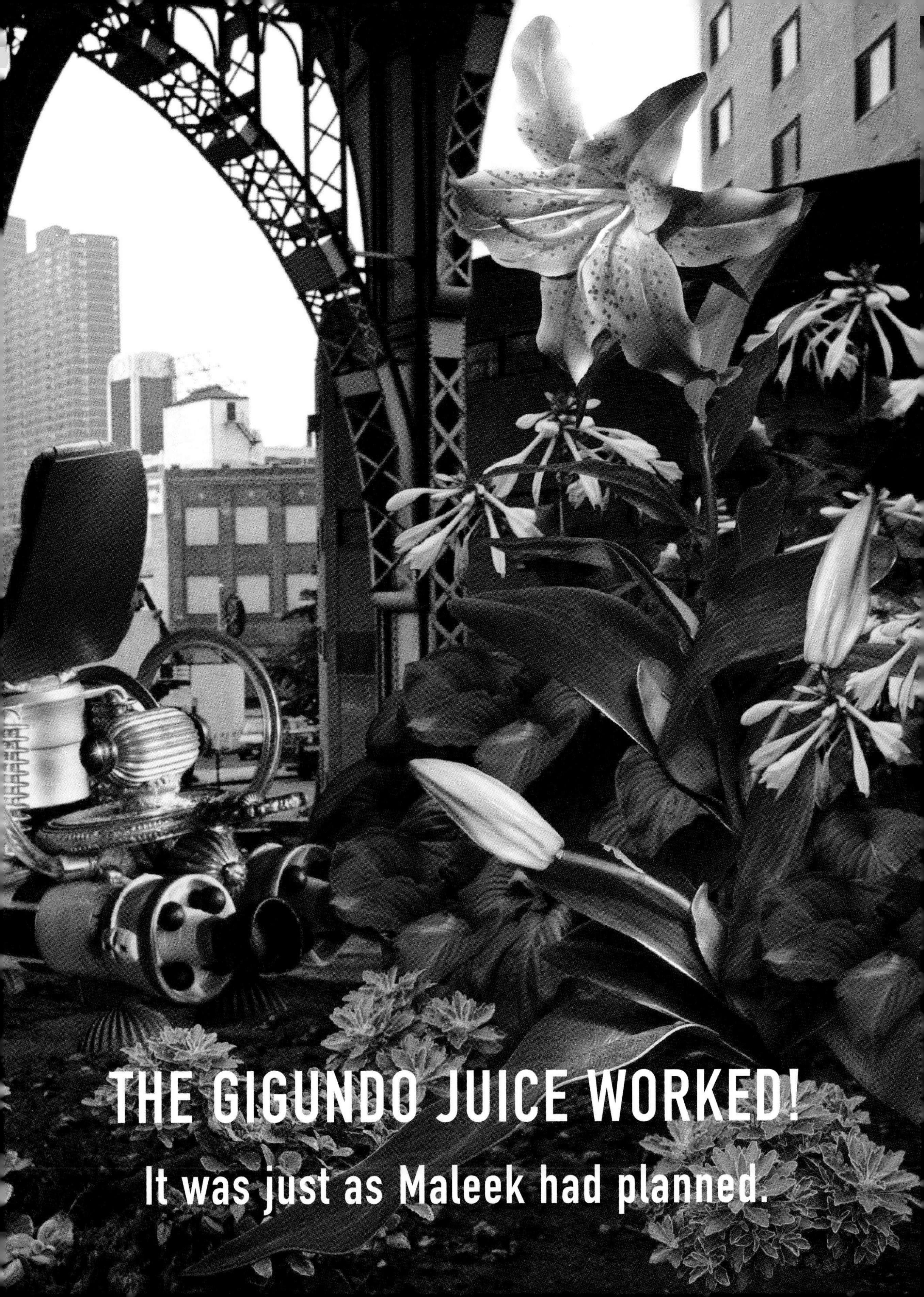

THE GIGUNDO JUICE WORKED!

It was just as Maleek had planned.

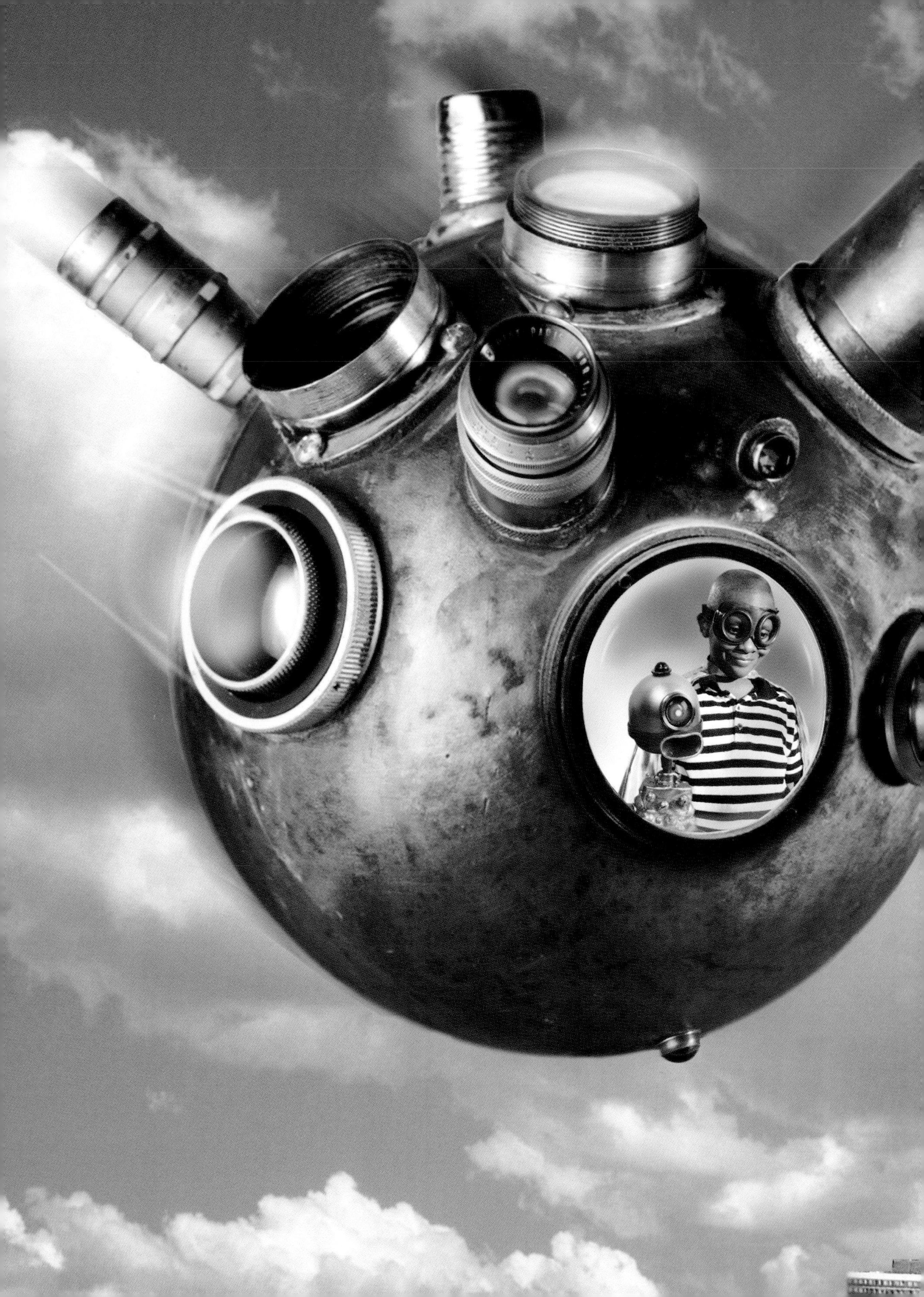

Maleek and Marvyn blasted off in their
soda pop-fueled GYROPOD.
They flew high above the city,
spreading GIGUNDO JUICE everywhere.

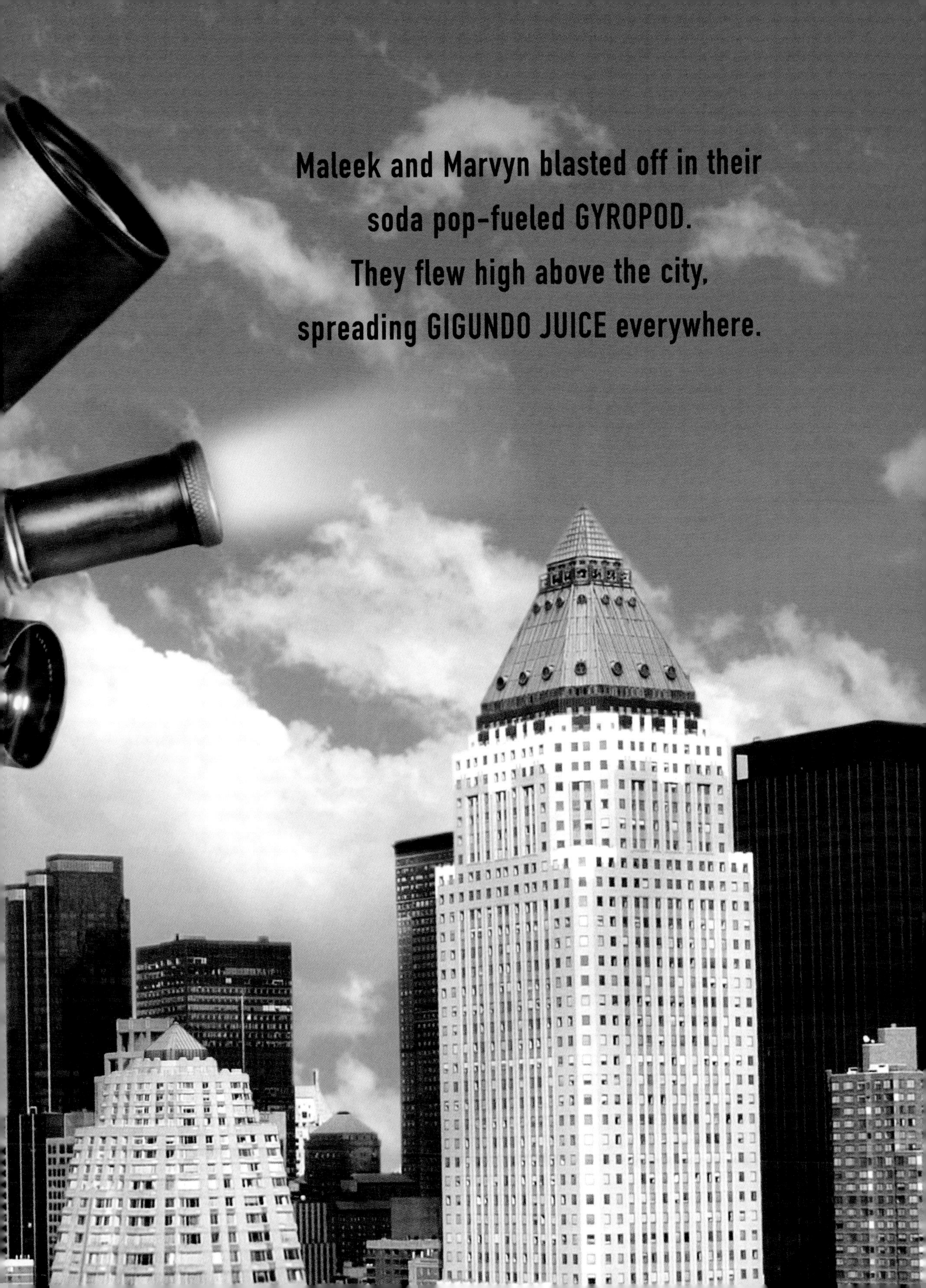

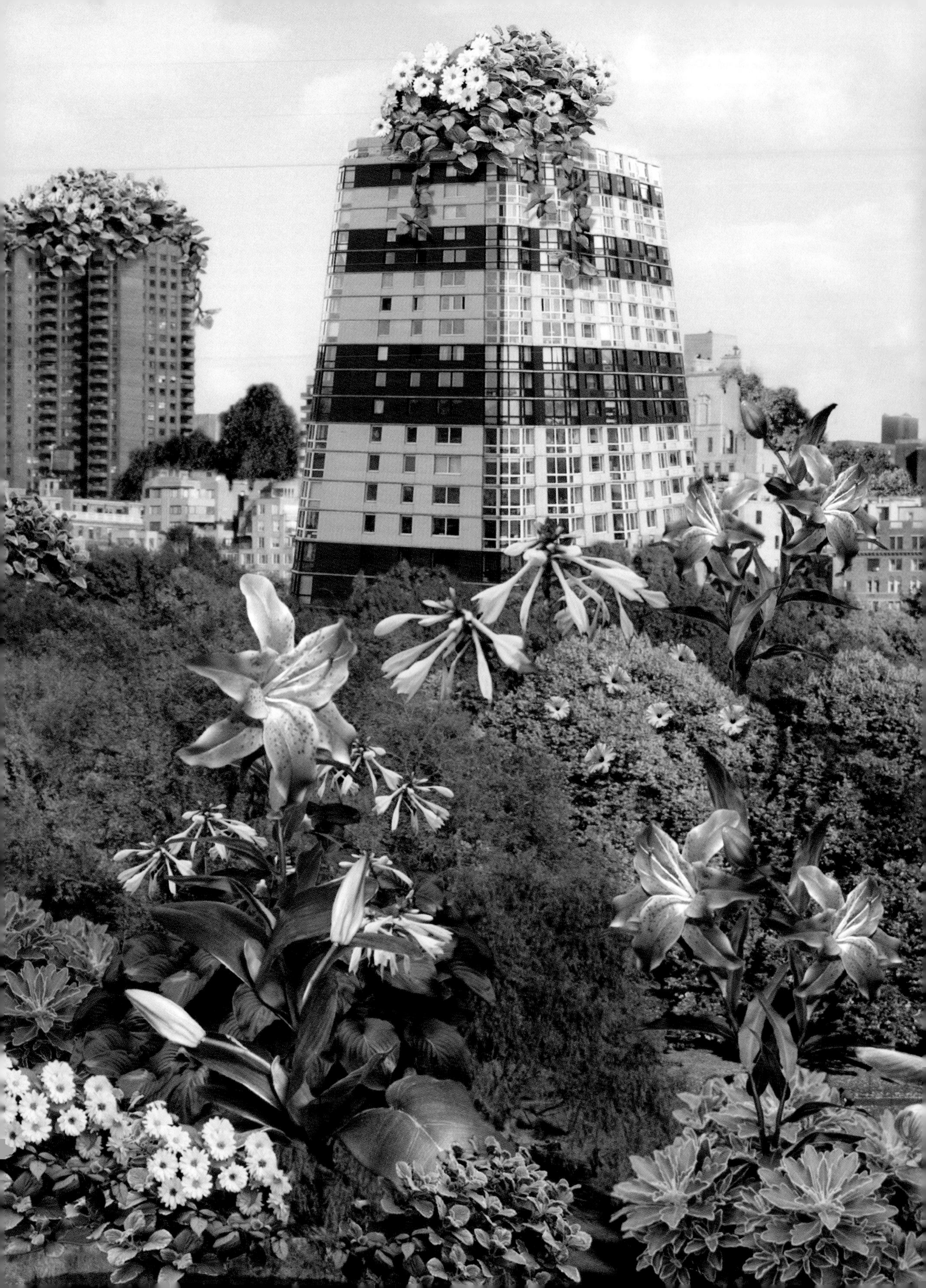

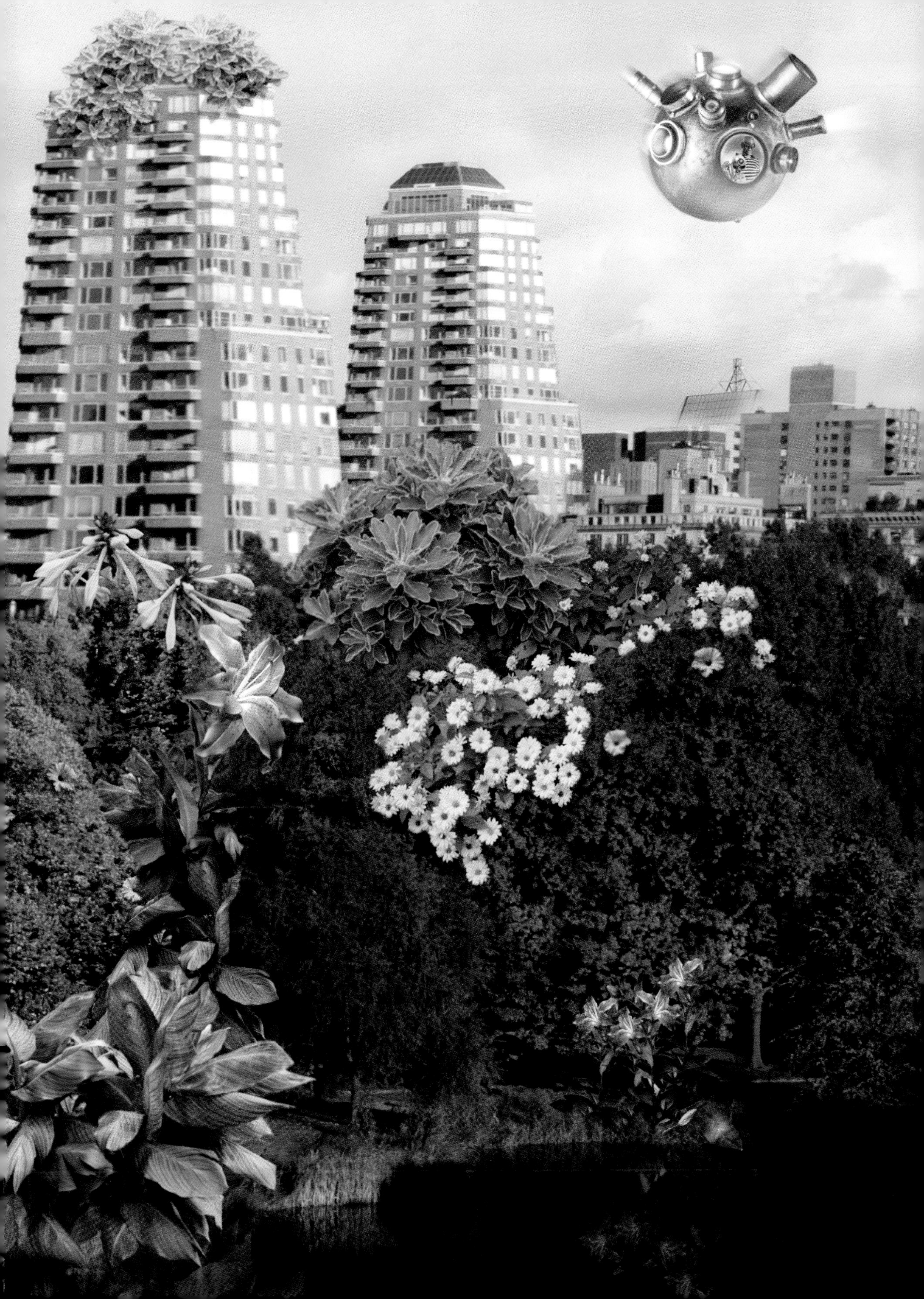

A superhero's work
was done . . .

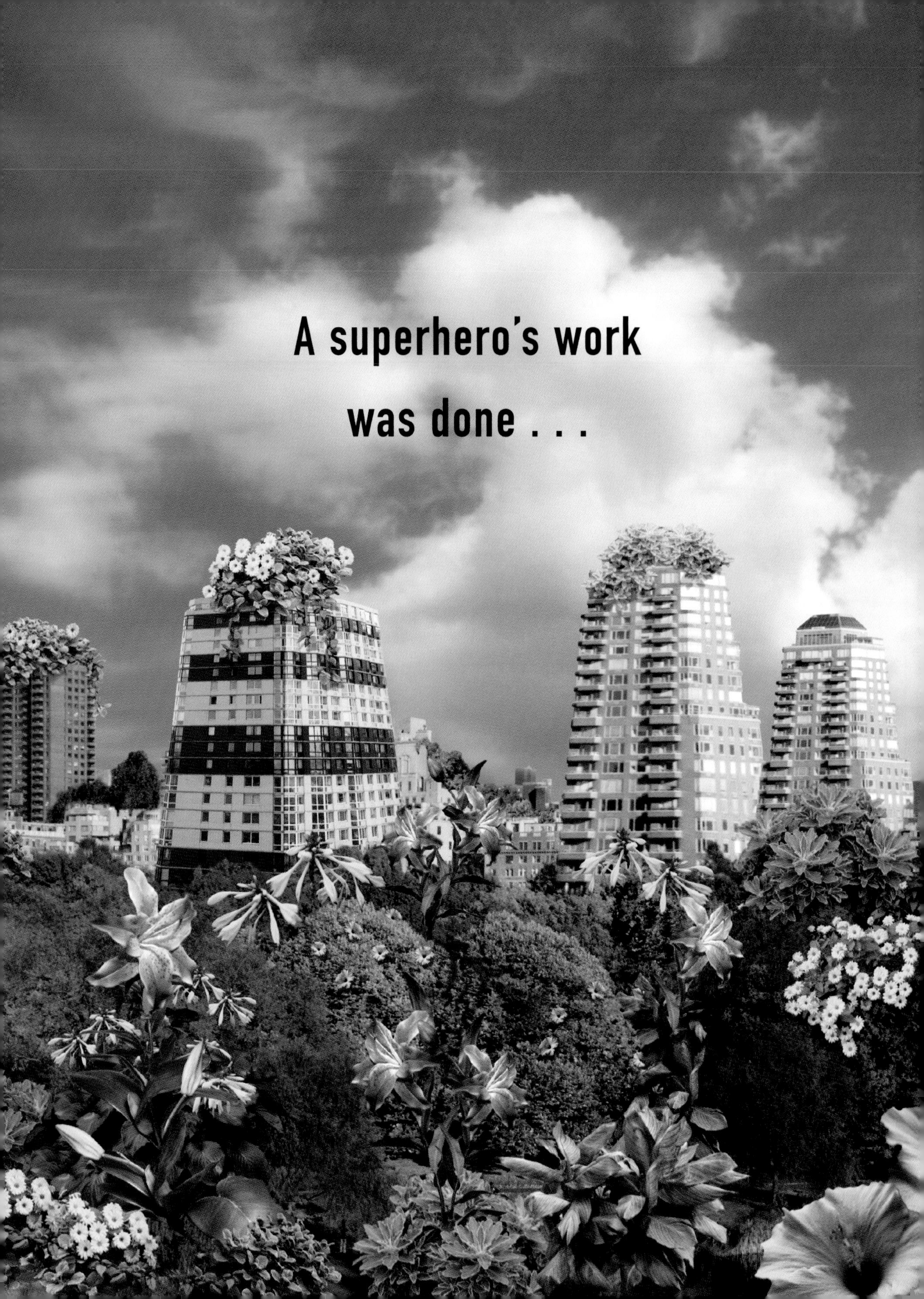

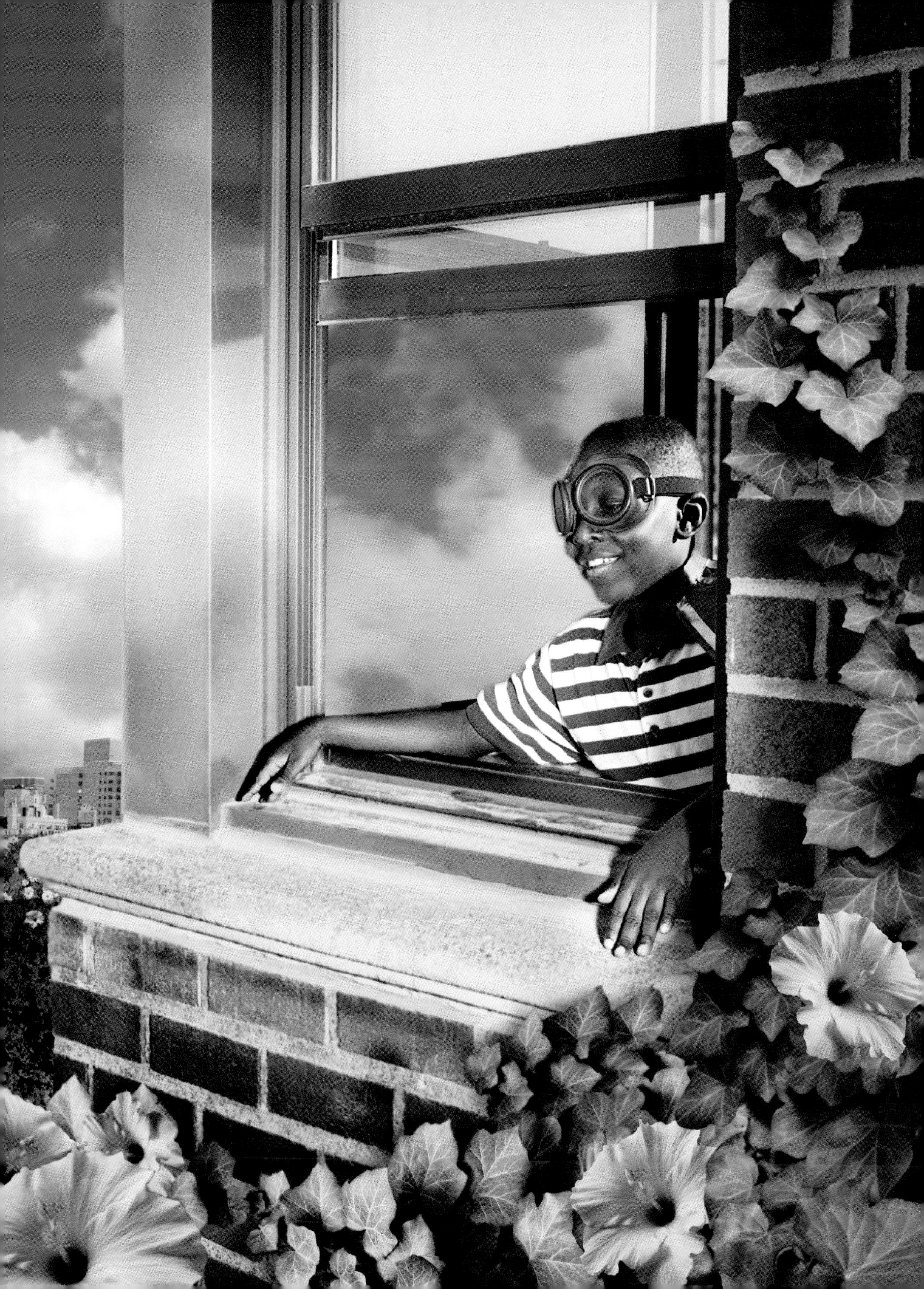

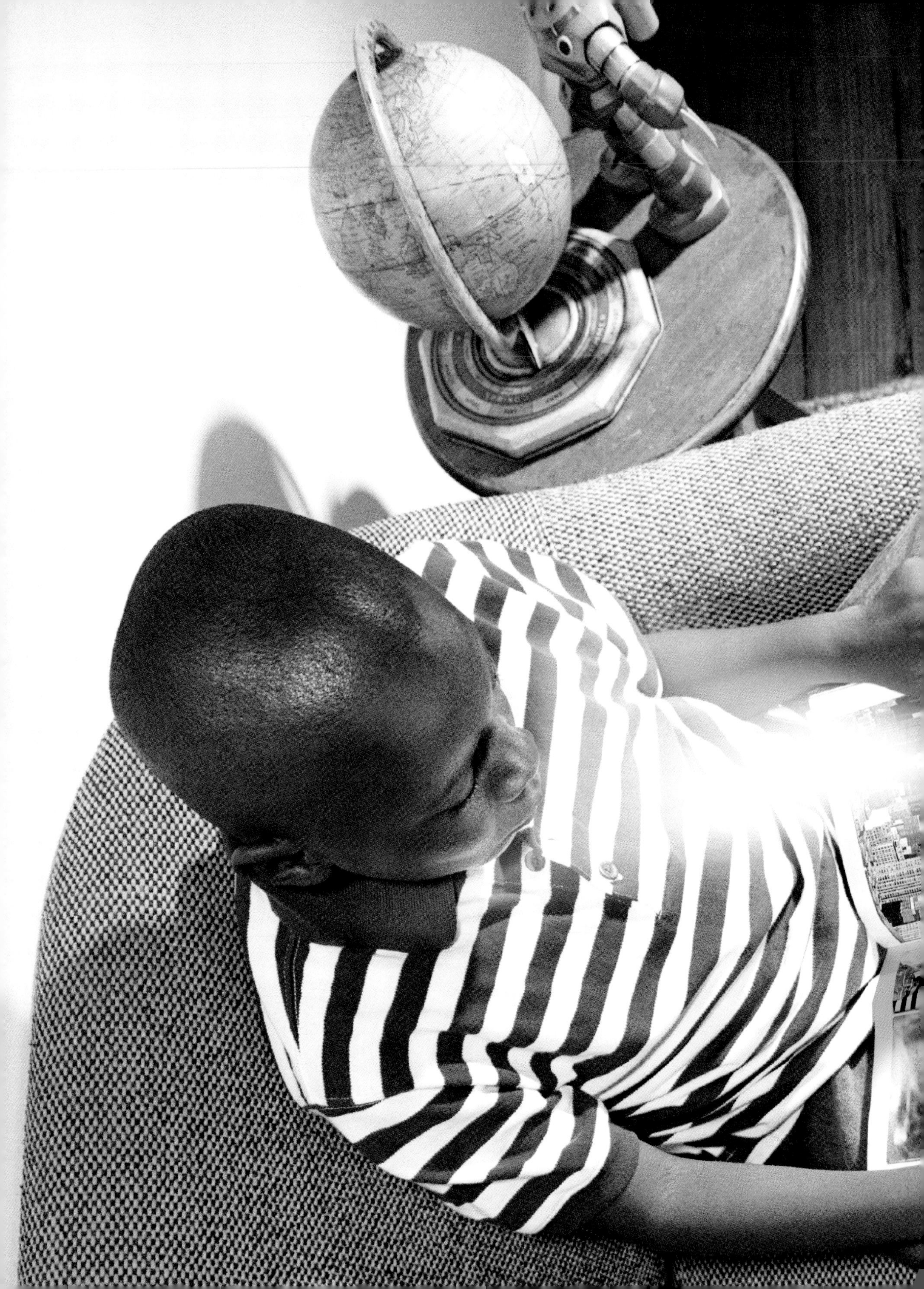

. . . at least for today.

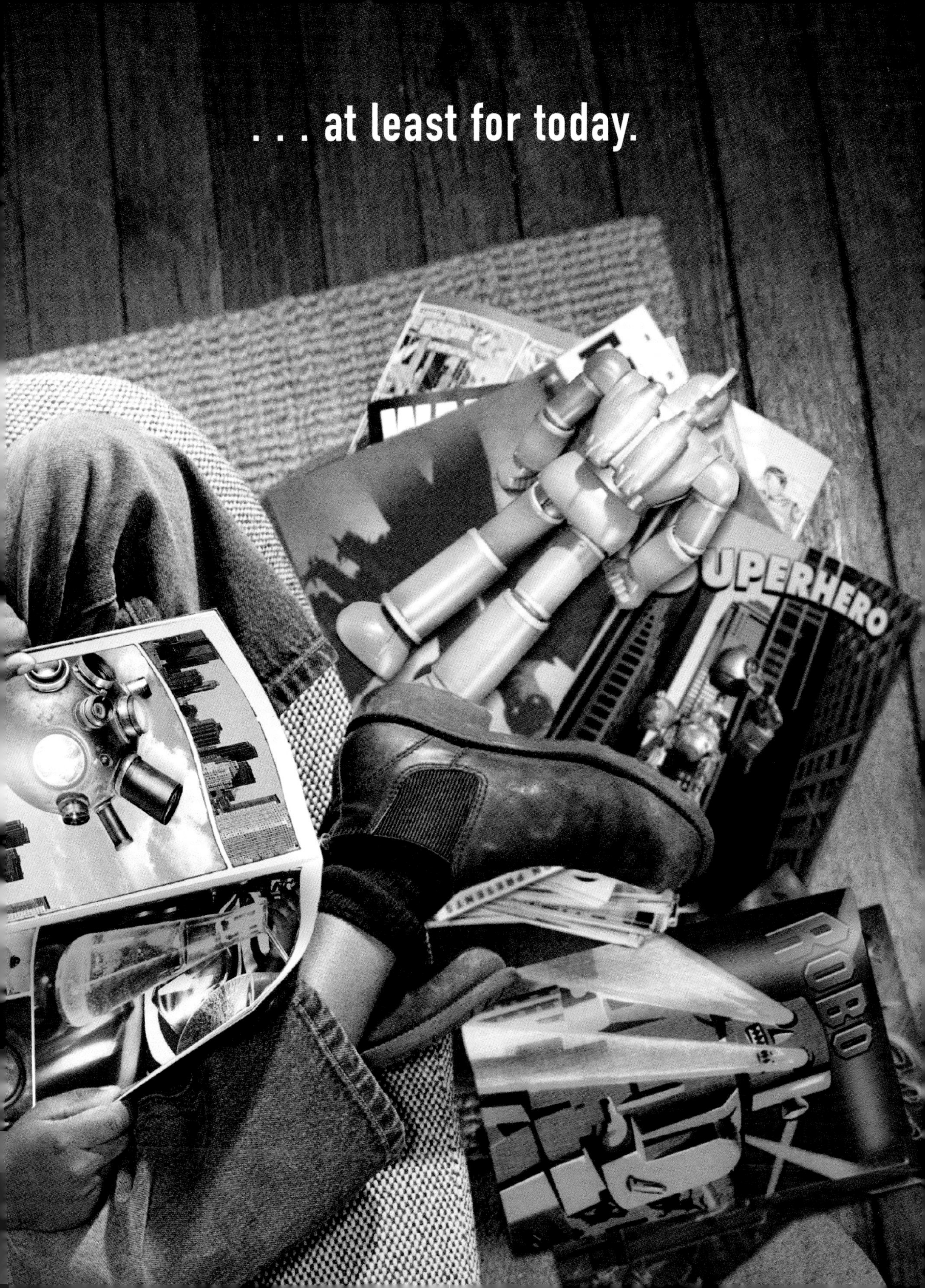
UPERHERO
ROBO

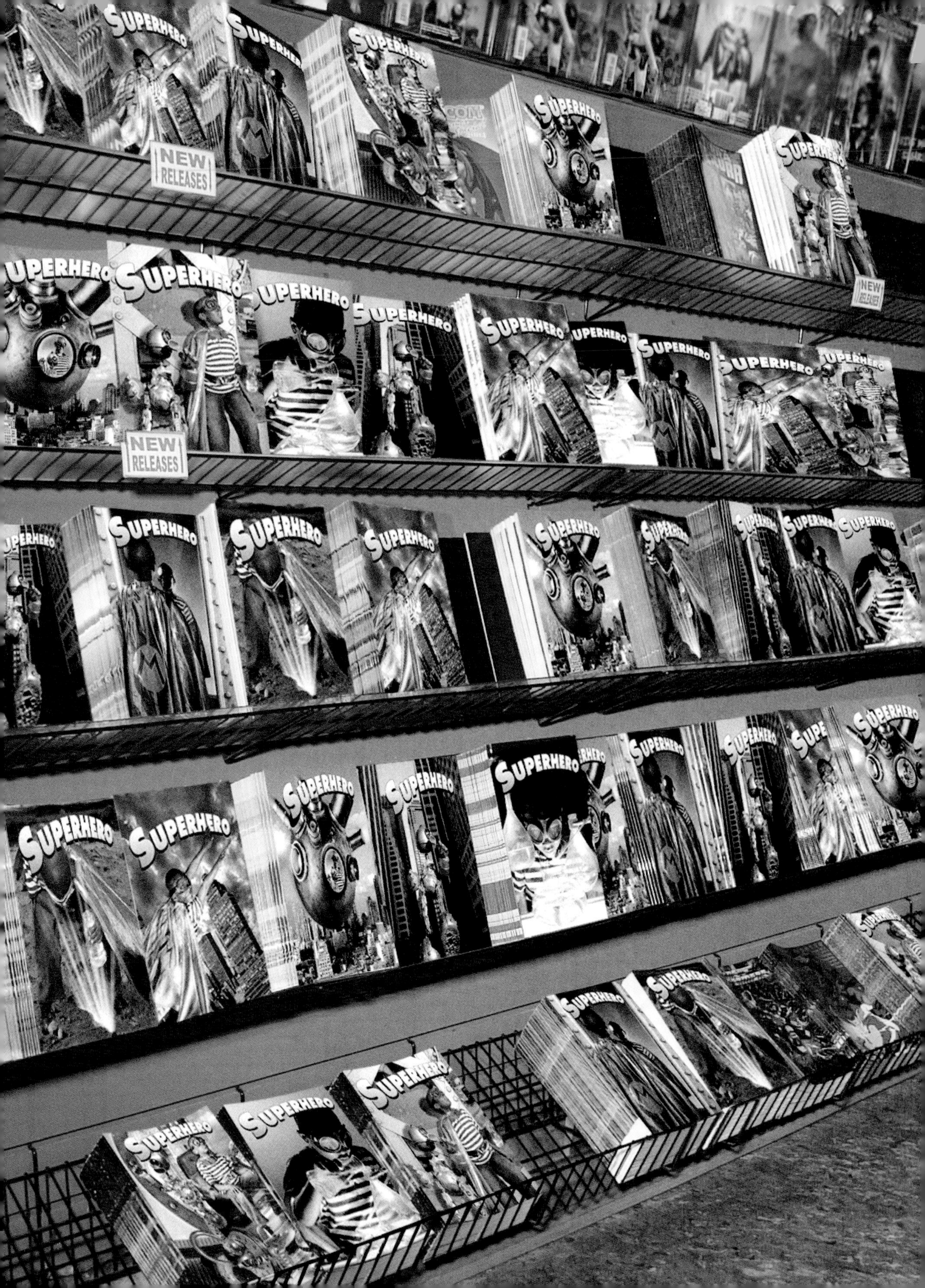
SUPERHERO
SUPERHERO
SUPERHERO
NEW
RELEASES
SUPERHERO
SUPERHERO
SUPERHERO
SUPERHERO
SUPERHERO
SUPERHERO
NEW
RELEASES
SUPERHERO
SUPERHERO
SUPERHERO
SUPERHERO
NEW
RELEASES
SUPERHERO
SUPERHERO
SUPERHERO
SUPERHERO
SUPERHERO
SUPERHERO
SUPERHERO
SUPERHERO
SUPERHERO
SUPERHERO
SUPERHERO
SUPERHERO
SUPERHERO
SUPERHERO
SUPERHERO
SUPERHERO
SUPERHERO
SUPERHERO